D0526892

MORE THINGS IN HEAVEN

I said, 'Henri! I just saw my brother — I saw Leon, right here in Quito!'

Chambord stared at me. Being French-born, he was too polite to tell me in so many words that I was insane, but I could see that it was a tough job.

'Calm yourself, David,' he instructed solicitously. 'A glass of water? A cigarette? You are all worked up.'

'Of course I am!' I snapped. I leaned on the edge of his desk and repeated my former statement, slowly and clearly. 'I just saw my brother, Leon, here in Quito!'

'It must have been someone else, David.'

I said, 'Hell! My own *brother*! I saw him right there on the Calle Gagarin, no more than ten minutes back!'

'At a distance, no doubt. You may have been thinking about your brother and fancied you saw a resemblance.'

'It's only two years since I saw Leon,' I cut in. 'We grew up in one another's pockets. I'm saying it isn't possible for me to be mistaken.'

But by this time I was having trouble convincing myself. Chambord sensed this and produced his ace of trumps.

'It is more than *possible*,' he said. 'It is certain. For your brother is aboard *Starventure*, and *Starventure* is crossing the orbit of Jupiter.'

Also by John Brunner
in Hamlyn Paperbacks

THE STARDROPPERS

TIMES WITHOUT NUMBER

MORE THINGS IN HEAVEN

JOHN BRUNNER

Hamlyn Paperbacks

MORE THINGS IN HEAVEN
ISBN 0 600 20262 3

First published in Great Britain 1983
by Hamlyn Paperbacks
Copyright © 1973 by Brunner Fact & Fiction Ltd

This book is based on an earlier work by the author
entitled *The Astronauts Must Not Land*,
Copyright © 1963 by Ace Books.

Hamlyn Paperbacks are published by
The Hamlyn Publishing Group Ltd.,
Astronaut House,
Feltham, Middlesex, England.

Printed and bound in Great Britain by
Collins Glasgow

68310561

01860532

1

I was still shaking as I walked into Chambord's office a good ten minutes afterward. Ramona, the pretty local girl who served as barrier between Chambord and the outside world, put her hand up to her open mouth as I went past her. Her eyes enormously wide, she said, *'Madre de Dios!'* Then she crossed herself rapidly. I looked as though I'd seen a ghost.

As far as I could tell, I *had* seen a ghost.

I caught Chambord at his desk when I opened his door. Behind him on the wall he had a giant blowup of the Andromeda Nebula — one of the famous series taken at the Lunar Observatory — so sited that when he sat upright it framed his head like a halo. I think he had it fixed that way on purpose. I half expected him to be angry at my marching in without knocking; instead, he was so proud of the fact that he recognized me after two years, he got right through his first sentence before he noticed the ghastly expression I was wearing. He said, 'If anyone had asked me to bet who would be first in here when it was time, I'd have said, "David Drummond, of course!" And — and in the name of the good God, David, what is wrong?' Catching on belatedly, he rose halfway to his feet. 'Is it that the altitude has overcome you?'

'Altitude be damned,' I said, and let myself fall into the visitor's chair, taking off my dark glasses so that I could wipe my sweating face. The fact that Quito is nine thousand feet up had no more to do with my fit of the shakes than the fact that it's on the equator had to do with my perspiring; I'd dutifully gulped down my day's ration of oxygen-utilization pills and would have been a fool not to. Yet I could feel my heart hammering my ribs to break them apart.

I said, 'Henri! I just saw my brother — I saw Leon, right here in Quito!'

Chambord stared at me. Being French-born, he was too polite to tell me in so many words that I was insane, but I

5

could see that it was a tough job.

'Calm yourself, David,' he instructed solicitously. 'A glass of water? A cigarette? You are all worked up.'

'Of course I am!' I snapped. I leaned on the edge of his desk and repeated my former statement, slowly and clearly. 'I just saw my brother Leon, here in Quito!'

'It must have been someone else, David.'

I said, 'Hell, my own *brother*! I saw him right there on the Calle Gagarin, no more than ten minutes back!'

'At a distance, no doubt. You may have been thinking about your brother and fancied you saw a resemblance.'

I drew a deep breath and let it out with deliberate patience; obediently, my heart went back to something nearer its normal tempo. I said, 'Have you any brothers yourself?'

'Ah . . . . Yes, I have two brothers.'

'Do you think you could mistake someone else for a brother of yours if you were no further from him than the width of the Calle Gagarin?'

'My brothers are in France; I have not see them for many years now. So —'

'It's only two years since I saw Leon,' I cut in. 'We grew up in one another's pockets. I'm saying it isn't possible for me to be mistaken.'

But by this time I was having trouble convincing myself. Chambord sensed this and produced his ace of trumps.

'It is more than possible,' he said. 'It is certain. For your brother is aboard *Starventure*, and *Starventure* is crossing the orbit of Jupiter.'

At that point my professional reflexes took over. I forgot the ridiculous notion that I could have seen Leon in Quito. I'd known all along that it must be an illusion. My mind jerked back to what Chambord had said when I came in: 'If anyone had asked me to bet who would be first in here when it was time . . .'

I had my crystal recorder — flat, the size of two packs of cigarettes — out of my pocket on the instant. I said, 'Since when? How long ago did they pick up her signal?'

'Only a little over an hour ago. I was working on the release when you came in.'

'Give me the bare facts. I'll be back for more later.'

He smiled, plainly relieved to see me acting more like my

6

usual self, and held out a regular UN message form. I'd learned to read space-code in my cradle, more or less — one glance was sufficient. *Starventure* had returned to normal space fifteen degrees above the plane of the ecliptic and five hundred million miles from the Sun; her direction of sublight travel was normal to Alpha Centauri and her signals were coming in strong and clear to say, 'Crew well and mission successful!'

'The biggest story since Columbus,' I said, handing back the form and getting to my feet. 'And I'm on to it ahead of the crowd. Maybe I should have myself tested for psi ability! Until I saw Leon — *thought* I saw,' I corrected myself as I noticed a disapproving curl of Chambord's lip — 'I hadn't the slightest intention of calling here today. When do they expect to make actual contact?'

'I have not yet been informed.' Chambord shrugged. 'It all depends, of course, on the resultant speed with which she re-entered normal space. If she is able to brake and turn under her own power in order to make the distance to Earth-orbit, then it may be as little as forty hours; if they need to send her tugs it might easily be longer than a week.'

'Fine! I'll be back!'

I went out in such a hurry I slammed the door, and the green United Nations shield on the outer side almost fell off its peg with the bang. Ramona jerked on her chair and glanced around, preparing to cross herself again; I gave her the most reassuring grin I could manage and headed for the pay phone-booths in the foyer.

I was probably the first man to profit directly from the launching of *Starventure*; I mean, naturally, apart from those who had salaried jobs on the project. At that time — two years before — I'd had a science-news column syndicated in about thirty countries through Solar Press and its associated agencies. It was pure luck that, owing to my inside position, which in turn I owed to having Leon for a brother, I had made a small fortune out of my coverage of the launching — or, if 'fortune' is too grandiose a word, what I counted as such: enough to turn freelance and concentrate on books instead of a grinding weekly schedule.

I remembered, as I waited in the phone-booth for my call to Solar Press's New York office to go through, how Hank

Sandler had received the news of my decision to leave his staff. I told him jokingly that he ought to be glad to see me go, because he was always complaining about my phone credit card. It was the most expensive the agency had ever guaranteed, being good for sound-and-vision A-1 priority calls from any place on Earth to New York. (Once I'd tried to get them to extend it to Luna, but with tight-beam satellite-relay calls running at twenty bucks a second, they refused. Anyhow, the trip to the Moon that I'd had in mind fell through at the last moment.)

So when I put the card in front of him, I expected him to try and talk me out of quitting. He did no such thing — just picked up the card and handed it back and said, 'Compliments of Solar Press.'

I'd never used it since, but I'd never gone anywhere without it. *Now* I felt I was entitled to use it again.

The face of one of the New York staff went up on the screen, and I fished in memory for the name: Jimmy Weston, that was it. He said, 'Thank goodness we reached you, Mr Drummond. Mr Sandler's been going half crazy.'

I blinked. I said, 'What do you mean, "you reached me?" Not that I know of, you didn't.'

'We've been paging you all over Venezuela. Isn't that where you're calling from?'

'Haven't been there since yesterday afternoon. Look, whatever it is you want me for can wait. Give me the copy desk — I have a clear beat, but it'll only last a few minutes.'

'I — I guess I'd better put you through to Mr Sandler.'

And before I could say any more, he did. Sandler's face came up on the screen just as he was breathing out a huge cloud of cigar smoke, and it hung frozen around his head until the next picture-melt was due.

I said, 'Hank, it's great to see you, but I didn't call for a social chat. I've been trying to tell Jimmy Weston that I have a monumental beat. Listen — *Starventure* is back!'

His voice was absolutely level as he answered. 'Maybe that accounts for it.'

This was so far from the response I'd been anticipating, I was completely taken aback. 'Accounts for what?' I said foolishly, and then recovered my sense of priorities. 'No, don't waste time explaining — just put me onto the copy desk!'

'Tell me instead.' I heard the rustle of paper; then the

8

picture-melt caught him with an open pad of paper and a pen.

I summed it up baldly, heard his message-tube click and knew that the information was on the way to the telefaxes. Stage one was safely over. The second stage would be to write the real story, but I'd been revising it in my head ever since the launching, and it would come out automatically.

'Thanks, David,' Sandler said after a pause. 'It's the biggest. How far ahead of the competition are you?'

'Not much more than a quarter hour, I guess. Henri Chambord is too strict for that. But it so happened I came into the UN press office here in Quito because I — '

I hesitated. Should I say, 'I saw my brother?' Or: 'I *thought* I saw my brother?'

I backed down. Part of me was still sure that it had been Leon I'd seen large as life in the bright noon sunlight. Part of me was perfectly aware that he was out near Jupiter's orbit.

'Well, the reason doesn't matter,' I concluded. 'It so happened I walked in on Henri just as he was drafting the press release. Coincidence. And, speaking of coincidence, how come you were trying to contact me? Have we all turned psychic?'

'Not exactly.' Sandler sounded puzzled. 'David, have you heard anything about the appearance of a monster in the sky over southern Chile? Panic in a fishing village down there?'

'No, not that I can recall. And if that's what you were after me to check up on, I ought to warn you mass hallucination isn't in my line.'

'You know me better than to think I'd send you chasing after a routine silly-season story, don't you?' Sandler let a trace of annoyance show in his tone. 'The point is, David, this doesn't — doesn't *smell* like a phony. It's too well documented; too many different accounts from various sources agree too closely on trivial details.'

I didn't try to argue. Hank Sandler might not be able to tell a nucleotron from an ergolyzer, but his instinct for what would make news bordered on the supernatural. All I said was, 'Do you still want me to check on it? Henri says I have at least forty hours before they make direct contact with the starship.'

'Heavens, no! You stay right where you are — and I'll

expect your first thousand words before I go out for lunch, okay?'

I chuckled; that sounded like the old Hank Sandler.

'But I'll get someone else to look into it,' he added, and my amusement faded.

'You don't think there could be some connection between it and the return of *Starventure?*' I suggested.

'I'm not going to make any off-the-top-of-the-head guesses,' he countered firmly. 'Anyway, the timing's wrong — this thing appeared last night, and you just told me *Starventure* got back an hour or so ago. Still . . .' He made chewing noises. 'Tell you what: I'll 'fax you the story care of the UN press office, and put in one or two other puzzling items as well, which have the same feel about them. You might at least find them provocative.'

Another picture shift caught him leaning back with a lugubrious expression which didn't match his warm voice as he concluded, 'Well, that's irrevelant. What I ought to be saying, of course, is thanks for remembering the old firm. But I don't seem to have enough words.'

'Save yours,' I said. 'I have plenty. Get me the copy desk and I'll write your main release over the phone.'

The picture wiped and a sign came on saying, 'Solar Press copytaking — please start talking at the third tone.' I closed my eyes. I didn't have to fumble, or work from notes — not on this story. I knew exactly what I needed to say and how it could best be said.

'A dream as old as civilization has come true. Man has thrown down his challenge to the stars . . .'

2

I was still talking when the door of the 'fax room across the foyer opened and a messenger headed for Chambord's office. He came back at a dead run, shouting and waving a sheet of paper. In the soundproof booth I couldn't hear what he was saying, and my Spanish — though reliable — was a trifle rusty. But I didn't have to hear a word to deduce

10

that inside half an hour every reporter in Quito from the agency men to the frowsiest legmen off the locals would be cramming themselves into this building the way they used to two years ago.

Two years ago . . .

I finished my dictation. Sandler came back to say that the bundle of material he'd promised me was on the 'faxes, and to thank me again, but now the storm was about to break in earnest, he had other things to attend to and there was no chance for casual chat. I signed off with a promise to call back in the evening and left the booth.

There was now going to be a long period of weary waiting until actual contact was made with the returning ship. I decided I might as well put myself in the mood by hanging around until the promised material from New York came through on the 'faxes. Regardless of how it compared with the news about *Starventure*, it would at least be interesting to see if I could work out why Sandler took it so seriously. Accordingly I sat down on one of the comfortable padded benches around the foyer to smoke a thoughtful cigarette and to worry again about the reason for my coming here today.

Damn it, after two years I couldn't not have known my own brother — not in bright sunlight across the width of a street! Yet all logic said I must have done just that. I'd seen Leon go aboard the ferry with my own eyes, and that ferry had lifted to *Starventure* orbiting at three thousand miles, and had snicked into the after hold — because it was going to serve as one of the landing-boats if Alpha Centauri turned out to have planets men could walk on.

Then the tugs had dragged the starship's vast hull out of orbit. I'd seen that, too — all of Earth had, on the planet-wide TV linkup covering the departure. Beyond Mars' orbit and slanting Centaurus-ward, the tugs had dropped off. Captain Rukeyser had called a nervous-sounding goodbye, and all the news commentators the following day had said how his nervousness was a wonderful reminder that after all it was ordinary men who were going to the stars.

And they went.

Where? How? Even to me — and I've spent my working life making science and technology comprehensible to the man in the street — it was a hell of a job putting the thinking

11

behind that stardrive into everyday language. Liu Chen, who laid the foundations for it, spoke nothing but his native Mandarin, and expounded his theories in symbology so abtruse more than one doctorate was awarded for theses clarifying it. I was once told by a linguistics expert whom I was interviewing that Liu Chen's nationality probably had a lot to do with this diffuculty; Chinese thinking, even after a century of writing with letters, was heavily conditioned by the structure of the Chinese language, he told me.

As simply as possible, though: Liu Chen developed a system for identifying individual particles by describing their relationship to other particles. He began with atoms, and in the general theory — which took him another ten years — extended his range to cover photons, mesons, the whole gamut down to and including neutrinos. Then he came most of the way back again and produced statistical tools for handling local relationships between substantial numbers of particles. He received a Nobel Prize, a United Nations award and a lifetime pension from the Chinese government, and retired to write a commentary on the book *I Ching* and yarrow-stalk divination.

Then a Chukchi Eskimo studying theoretical physics in Ljubljana and a Mexican at Columbia independently saw what Liu Chen had overlooked: that one of the characteristics he had proposed for identifying individual particles could be isolated from the rest, since it depended on the location of other particles so distant that they were effectively at infinity. And if this characteristic were real, then it could be altered by the application of certain local stresses in the continuum.

On that fragile foundation they built a robot ship which crossed the Solar System four times as fast as the radio signal announcing it had been launched. And next they built *Starventure*.

When Rukeyser hit the stardrive control, every atom of the ship and its crew, plus the associated energy, shifted into a different state of being. The ship's 'proper' location, so to speak, became somewhere in the vicinity of Alpha Centauri — and there it went, simply because it 'wanted' to belong to our ordinary universe again and until it was in the right place it couldn't.

It was clearer in mathematical symbols. The same linguist who told me about Liu Chen's Chinese though<sup>

patterns, also predicted that in another century we'd cheerfully be describing stardrive operation verbally. 'What's more,' he went on, 'we'll be using words we use already. We'll simply understand different conceptual referents for them.'

I asked him to give me an example, and he suggested, 'Take the word "engine." Originally that meant the same as "gadget" or "contrivance." Now it's taken over the meaning of "motor" and extended it.'

But when I put that in my weekly column, almost a hundred people wrote in to say they didn't believe it.

I was *sure* I'd seen Leon!

It wasn't as though we were brothers in the same way as Henri Chambord and his brothers — Henri happily settling in Quito, going home on vacation maybe once in three or four years, the others content to stay in France, where they'd been born. Leon and I were six years apart in age, but we'd always been exceptionally close. Since my father disappeared when I was twelve, and my mother died when I was nineteen, I'd had to be as much a parent as a brother to him.

I was studying physics and chemistry, but when Mom died I quit and went to work on a small-town paper, where I found that enough of what I'd learned in the lab had stuck for me to consider becoming a science writer, which I did. In the end I worked up to a Kalinga Prize and the top post in the business — on roving assignment for Solar Press — and ultimately was able to settle to a comfortable living from two popular-scientific books a year.

Possibly it was hero worship that persuaded Leon to take up the physical sciences, or maybe I influenced him in his choice through my hangover of bitterness at having had to forgo a career in research. However it arose, he developed a strong yen to carry on where I'd left off, and it turned out he had the gift. His was one of the doctorates awarded for theses clarifying Liu Chen's theories, and thanks to that he applied for, and got, a job with the team designing *Starventure's* drive. And eventually they picked him as crew.

They allowed only the crew's immediate families and fiancées to see them board the ferry before departure, but since the crew numbered sixty, that was a fair-sized crowd. I was Leon's one close relative, of course, and I was proud

13

as hell. About the only thing I was prouder of was the story I wrote afterwards. Virtually everyone present sold their first-person impressions to some agency, to be ghosted for publication, but I was a reporter, and I was there, and the fact showed, and people could tell. I made my pile, left Quito, and set out to enjoy the rest of my life.

Now, back in the foyer of the UN press office, I could close my eyes and recapture the exact scene on that epochal day two years earlier. I could see Rukeyser with his vast black beetling eyebrows; I could see the almost womanish grace of Chandra Dan; I could see Hobart and Efremov and Soo. Above all, I could see Leon.

Alongside that recollection I could put the memory of the man I'd seen this very day, and make a point-for-point match right down to the expression on his features.

What were the odds against that? I did some inaccurate mental calculations involving the total population figure and the per-generation mixing of the genetic pool, and came up with something around ten to the seventh power. Multiplied by the number of cities on Earth and the number of days in my lifetime — because this had happened today in Quito and nowhere else — the result became altogether ridiculous.

So the hell with 'odds against'; they didn't enter the matter. More rational would be to assume my mind had played a trick on me. But why this particular trick on this particular day, which had brought me a piece of luck I craved more than anything else, a clear beat on the news of the starship's return? I'd joked to Chambord about being psychic, but I had little patience for ESP enthusiasts, and all the tests I'd had to undergo in the course of my job had shown me not to possess any detectable super-normal talent.

I assured myself firmly I was making too much out of a coincidence. Thinking that I'd seen Leon could be ascribed to simple association of ideas and could as easily have happened yesterday or the day before. After all, I didn't come very frequently to Quito, even though it was the spatial capital of Earth, chosen as such for several excellent reasons. To start with, it was on the equator near as damn it; it was over nine thousand feet high, so there was that much less air for ascending ships to batter through (though they had been compelled to slide a couple of small mountains into the adjacent valleys to make enough level ground for the spaceport); and, not least important, it was in a country small enough not to make the conceited big powers jealous of their national honour. Everyone could feel patronizing and patting-on-head, barring a handful of other nations on this same continent, and as no one had been listening to their complaints lately, they appeared to be giving up.

I'd got to know it pretty well two years ago. On the two or three occasions I'd been back in the interim, I hadn't noticed many changes. But if *Starventure's* mission had been really successful, there would be other trips, and other ships, and this city would be altered wholly out of recognition.

The door of the 'fax room opened again. There was now a sound of jubilation from inside, and I distinctly heard the clink of bottles mixed up with the purring hum of facsimile transmitters and receivers. A girl emerged with a thick sheaf of the light brown heat-sensitive paper they use on the 'faxes, glanced around, and came over to inquire if I was the Señor Drummond.

I assured her I was and accepted the packet she handed me. There was far more here than I'd expected; Sandler must be taking his hunch extremely seriously. Included were not only Solar Press stories but releases from rival agencies and even clips from papers which must have been cut out and put straight in the transmitter, for I could see the shadowed edges where the clipper's scissors had gone off a straight line.

Frowning, I leafed through them. Before I got halfway I was beginning to wonder whether Hank Sandler's nose for a news story had at long last led him down a blind alley. I couldn't for the life of me see why he had been so impressed as to make him page me – quoting Jimmy Weston – 'all over Venezuela.'

The first two items were accounts of the phenomenon he'd mentioned on the phone – the panic-stricken fisherfolk of a Chilean coastal village had reported seeing a vast gape-jawed animal face luminous in the sky. I thought at first glance they were duplicates and was going past the second one when a name struck me and I checked back. In fact they weren't duplicates. One was from a village called

15

Mochasia, the other from a place called San Felipe. They agreed on a remarkable number of essential points, but they'd been put on the wires by different agencies.

But an obvious explanation for them was right here in the third item Sandler had included, concerning an extraordinary display of the Northern Lights. If there had been auroral phenomena around the South Pole as well last night, that would account for everything very neatly. I myself had seen auroral displays that resembled stage curtains, rainbows and many other things; there was no reason why an overactive imagination shouldn't turn them into animal faces, too.

The remainder of the various stories included here could easily be related to the same source: violent electrical storms, blanking out of radio transmission over the central and southern Pacific, reports of peculiar magnetic anomalies from widely separated observatories . . .

I must have been paying attention with only half my mind, for it wasn't until I'd read the whole pile through a second time that I jolted in my seat and cracked my fingers in exasperation at my own dullwittedness. Ordinarily, one would associate phenomena like these to a solar storm or flare — yet I knew perfectly well we were currently in a Quiet Sun period. Hell, it was precisely because I was intending to include a chapter on recent solar studies in my next book that I'd come to Quito; one of the world's most famous solar observatories was a few miles down the road, and I had an appointment lined up to see its director.

But suppose these items Sandler had sent me were after all linked to the return of *Starventure* — say there were energies analogous to Cherenkov radiation preceding the emergence . . .

I'd certainly have to inquire about that possibility. But not right now. Catching sight of a wall clock across the foyer, I realized I was going to be late for my lunch date, and that I declined to do, starships notwithstanding. Pocketing the bundle of papers, I made for the exit, and was almost knocked off my feet by the rush of newsmen coming in answer to Chambord's press release.

As I headed for the restaurant I reflected on the nature of luck.

3

I almost got married once, but we changed our minds and I thought afterwards it was just as well. What with Leon and family troubles, I put in a good deal of kid-minding early in life and never felt much that way inclined again. My old man's example didn't equip me as a satisfactory father, and on top of that my roving job made the idea seem pretty silly anyway.

But I'd met a good few good women who liked me on those terms, and the second thing I'd done on arriving in Quito had been to call Carmen. The first, naturally, had been to fix my appointment with the man I'd actually come to see. I wouldn't have made a trip to Quito specially to visit Carmen . . . but now I was about to see her, I was – as usual – wondering why not.

One member of *Starventure's* crew was Ecuadorian: a geologist-geophysicist called Hermanos Iglesias. He had two grandparents living, both parents, four uncles with wives and children, two aunts with husbands and one without, two brothers married with children, four sisters married with children and one married without children and one not married. They all came down to the ferry under the 'close relatives' clause, bubbling with happiness and boasting to everyone about their marvellous boy Hermanos who had won scholarships all through from first grade to university and was now going to the stars. Intermittently they invoked St Christopher.

Carmen was the unmarried sister. She was small, not at all pretty, with a sharp nose, a wry mouth, skin very faintly tinged with yellow and hair as black as space. She managed to get separated from the rest of the family in the crowd at the farewell ceremony, and I managed to catch up with her for long enough to make a date. I never figured out what it was that made her say yes, but whatever it was, I was grateful for it. I told her later that her ancestry must be one-quarter each Spanish, Irish, Amerind and puma, and she answered, 'No, not puma. I think jaguar.'

So that was always the second matter I had to attend to when something brought me to Ecuador. Sometimes I wished I came more often, and other times I told myself I ought to stay away for five years. However, a total stay of about a month and a half in two years wasn't exactly monopolizing her company.

She was in the bar of the restaurant when I got there, drinking iced passionfruit juice, and on the faces of the men present was the inevitable puzzled look as though they were wondering why they should go on staring at this girl who obviously wasn't in any sense beautiful.

Of course, the first thing I said after greeting her was, 'Have you heard?'

She raised one very black eyebrow, her forehead wrinkling into parallel ridges, and signalled the waiter to bring a drink for me.

'*Starventure* is back!' I said.

She took the news as calmly as though I'd said, 'The sun is out today.' She sipped at her own drink before answering.

'So that explains it,' she said.

I had a momentary sense of dislocation; this was so like Hank Sandler's reaction to the news.

'Explains what?'

'My thinking I saw Hermanos this morning.'

I was just picking up the drink the waiter had set before me. The shock of her remark made me jump as though I'd been stabbed and I nearly lost my grip on the condensation-slippery sides of the glass. I said, 'You saw your brother? Where? When?'

She made a casual gesture. 'Oh, I imagined that I saw him from my bedroom window this morning. I knew it could only be a vision, of course, and the fact that the ship is coming back would account for it. There has often been second sight in my family. My grandmother says it came from Ireland. Besides, I am the seventh child of a seventh child.'

Still as calm as could be, she sipped her drink again.

I took a deep breath. I said, 'I haven't any Irish in me, and I never heard that any of my Scots forebears were fey. I'm not even a seventh child — we haven't had such big families for generations. But . . .'

I hesitated, unable to screw up the courage to make the

foolish-sounding admission I'd intended, until something in her piercing dark eyes forced me to complete the statement.

I said finally, feebly, 'I saw Leon today.'

'You too?'

'You saw Leon as *well* as Hermanos?'

'No, no, no!' she laughed. 'I mean, you had a vision of your brother just as I did of mine. How strange!'

'Strange!' I said and swallowed my drink in one gulp in case she had any more shocks in store for me and next time I didn't retain my grip on the glass. 'I was so convinced it was really Leon, I went straight to the UN press office all set to accuse Henri Chambord of conspiring to deceive the public!'

'How "deceive"?'

'Why, if I'd seen Leon here with my own eyes, that must have meant either that *Starventure* had already returned and the news was being kept secret, or else she'd never gone anywhere in the first place and the whole project was a vast hoax.' I signalled the waiter as he passed again. Almost embarrassed, I added, 'I didn't think it far enough through to work out why anyone should want to perpetrate a hoax on that scale. I think my horse-sense belatedly caught up with me. I mean, the moment I heard the news from Henri I realized I must have suffered a hallucination.'

'David, you still don't really believe that,' she said quietly. 'My vision also seemed perfectly real. Are you hungry, or shall we go find out whether anyone else with relatives aboard the ship has seen them today?'

That was another shock — this time, a negative one: that she could conceive such an idea and prepare to act on it. She was completely serious; she was already reaching for the gloves and purse which the somewhat old-fashioned firm she worked for preferred their lady employees to display during business hours.

But it was in keeping with the rest of her, of course.

I put my hand on top of her purse an instant before her fingers touched it. I said, 'The hell with that. Yes, I'm very hungry. Also, I haven't seen you in months and I want to know what's news. Also I haven't much time right now — this afternoon I have to go and interview a professor, and my old boss at Solar Press has sent me a bunch of material I've got to study up on before I actually see the guy because

I think it contains some extra questions for me to put to him.' I half-drew the sheaf of 'fax paper from my pocket.

'Very well.' She gathered her belongings and rose. 'Shall we go in?'

We went into the restaurant and were shown to the table she'd reserved for us. I'd never been here before — Carmen had suggested the place when I called her up this morning. It was plushy and gilded, and there was a band which I found rather irritating, but the food and wine proved to be excellent.

'You asked me what is news,' Carmen said. 'You know I still have the old job, since you called me at the office. But I have my own apartment now. I would have told you on the phone, but each time you are away I think maybe you will change, so I preferred to see you face to face before mentioning it.'

'And have I changed?'

'You? No!' She wrinkled her nose amusingly. 'You will have dinner with me at home tonight? This is to cause scandal, of course, if my family learns of it. And will you be here long enough to call on them?'

I had to smile. 'You don't change, either,' I said. 'You remain exactly as astonishing as always.'

'You,' she retorted, 'are not astonishing at all. Always you come here for some excellent reason — an interview, a visit to some laboratory — and always you talk about it first and me second. That's the reason I like you. Most men talk about themselves first and go right on talking.'

'If I didn't know better, I'd think you didn't like men,' I said. The memory of how much better I did know startled me as I spoke, and I found myself wondering how I ever managed to stay away from Quito, the place where there was Carmen.

I decided to change the subject.

'As to how long I'm staying . . . Well, now *Starventure* is back, indefinitely. I'd intended three days at the most, but I promised Hank Sandler long ago that I'd cover the ship's return for him, and even if they hadn't contracted to pay ten thousand a week for as long as it takes — quarantine landing, debriefing, whatever — I'd still stay right here. After all, my brother's on board, and not everyone is going to have the chance to hear at first hand what the firs

20

star-trip was like.'

It still had power to make my voice shake a little, fill my guts with a chill of awe. *The first starship is back!* I repeated the words to myself under my breath. Then I said aloud, 'Carmen, doesn't it excite you, thinking of the sheer scale of the whole thing? More than eight light-years there and back, men circling under a different sun . . . Doesn't it?'

She fixed me squarely with the pools of midnight she had for eyes. She said in a level voice, 'I saw Hermanos this morning, David. I have never experienced second sight before. Nor have you. I believe in it. You don't. I'm — worried.'

I drove her back to her office after arranging to find my way to her new apartment for dinner at seven-thirty — and later rather than earlier, she said, if I didn't want to interfere with her cooking. I wished very much there was something I could say as we parted that might ease her troubled mind.

But I couldn't think of anything that made any sense.

It was then nearly time for me to start for the solar observatory, but before setting out I called Chambord and learned that there was nothing to add to the story I'd filed earlier, except that they were going to have to bring the ship in by tug. Orbits for ten tugs were being computed and their crews were on standby. I asked about human interest on the members of those crews and was told that there would be names and biographies going out by evening, but that until *Starventure* was safely in orbit around Mother Earth, space-radio traffic was going to be too heavy for frills like personal interviews with tug pilots.

Fair enough. I returned to my car and headed out of the city in the direction opposite to the spaceport. I was a good distance along the road to the observatory when I realized that I'd omitted to do precisely what I'd told Carmen I intended to — to wit, rethink completely the questions I was going to put to the astronomer I was due to visit. It was clear that my current book was about to be shelved in favour of ghosting Leon's first-person reminiscences of the journey to Alpha Centauri. But this was no reason at all to waste a prearranged appointment with an internationally known scientist; by tomorrow there would be reporters waiting on line outside every laboratory and observatory on Earth. I trod hard on the gas pedal, letting the wind of my passage blow away the questions I'd been meaning to ask and substitute some more topical ones.

I didn't think these were going to be so easy to answer.

4

Naturally I'd often heard of Professor Rodrigo Acosta, but I'd never met him before — which made him something of an exception among scientists of planetary standing. He had taken over as director of the observatory since my last visit to Ecuador. He received me in the same office as his predecessor, and I noted that he'd kept the same decorations: a blow up of a satellite picture showing a Pacific typhoon brewing, so perfect it looked like an artist's impression rather than the real thing, and a magnificent full-colour photograph of the solar corona during an eclipse, round the edge of which Bailey's Beads stood out like a fine pearl necklace.

He was a little dry man in shirtsleeves, who wore gold-rimmed glasses and spoke very good English. That didn't surprise me; according to *Who's Who in Science* he'd worked at both Flagstaff and Greenwich.

'I have been trying to reach you all the morning,' he began when I was seated. 'Since the news about the starship, I am being plagued by reporters who seem to think I have a private line into Captain Rukeyser's cabin, so I had intended to cancel our appointment. But since you are here . . .' He shrugged. 'Well, let me say there is none among your colleagues for whom I would prefer to have to make the exception.'

He took his glasses off rapidly, grinned and blinked at me, and put them on again. I thanked him sincerely; I'd trade a hundred compliments from laymen for one from a working scientist.

'And now,' he went on, 'what is it you wish to discuss? You had planned, according to your letter, to inquire about our latest solar data, but after the news of the starship I imagine you'd rather talk about that first. Not, I must warn you, that I will have a great deal to tell you.

I looked thoughtfully down at the crystal recorder I had on my knee, as usual, during my interviews. I had the impression that Acosta didn't entirely approve of my recording him, but couldn't think of grounds for an objection.

'As a matter of fact,' I said, 'I want to talk about both your latest solar data and the starship. We're in the middle of a Quiet Sun period right now, aren't we? So why should there be sudden violent solar activity at just this time?'

His face told me, before his voice, that my stab in the dark had found its target. I made a mental note to thank Sandler; once again his nose for news had proved correct.

With obvious reluctance, Acosta said, 'Well, yes, it is true that for the past day the Sun has been exceptionally active, but only for this stage of the sunspot cycle, you understand.'

'Active in what way? Fluctuations in the corona? Flares, magnetic anomalies, that kind of thing?'

'Yes, all of those.'

'Could there be a connection between this and the emergence of the starship into normal space?'

'I suppose there *could*,' he agreed with reluctance. 'It is naturally far too early to do more than make guesses, so please do not go away and tell the world that there is a connection. But . . . Well, while we can't rule out coincidence, we have to remember that this is the first time such a massive body has returned to normal space after so long a trip. Except, of course, when the ship arrived at Alpha Centauri, and the light which will inform about that has still a good three years to spend on its way here.'

'I seem to recall the suggestion being made that energies anologous to Cherenkov radiation might precede a body driven faster than light. Have you any comment on the idea?'

'No such radiation was detected, that I know of, during the testing of the robot ship which preceded *Starventure*. But certainly a − an influx of energy might account for the sudden burst of solar activity we're experiencing.' He hesitated. 'My turn to ask you a question, Mr Drummond. From whom did you learn about this unusual solar activity? I'd not have thought it sufficiently newsworthy to feature in the newspapers or on television.'

23

'It isn't. But some of its consequences have been.' I handed him the pile of material Sandler had 'faxed to me. While he was thumbing through the pile, I ran over my half-formulated idea.

Cherenkov radiation: the result of passing particles at extremely high speed through a substance in which they were effectively exceeding the speed of light. Compare it to ripples produced on water by the passage of a ship; as well as the wake astern, there are also ripples running ahead of the actual vessel. Theory said that a ship driven faster than light could not be reacting with objects in real space because the latter were in a different order of existence. But surely — I'd always intuitively balked at the dogmatic certainty of that assertion — if the ship could 'find its way' to a definite location in real space, there must be if not a connection, then at least an *association* with the normal universe. Particularly when it was slowing down, crossing that indefinable threshold between its two possible states of being, it must . . .

I roused myself to the realization that Acosta was handing back my papers.

'A well-educated guess, hm?' He sighed. 'The reasoning is clear, I think — blackout of radio communications, a panic due to some strange lights in the sky, brilliant displays of the aurorae, *et voilà*: you correctly deduce the bout of hiccups afflicting Old Man Sol. I am most impressed, though, by the speed with which you have news from such widely scattered sources delivered to you in a foreign country!'

'Oh, that's none of my doing,' I admitted. 'It was the New York bureau chief of the firm I used to work for who put this bunch together. At first I thought he was talking nonsense, but on reflection I decided he was absolutely right.'

I had been going to move on to a whole series of further questions, but I was forestalled by the shrilling of a phone on Acosta's desk. With a murmured apology he reached for the come-in switch.

The sound from the speaker was directionalized, so that I caught only a blurred word here and there. The importance of the message, though, could be read on his face, which registered first annoyance at the interruption, then surprise, and finally unaccountable gravity.

24

He ended the conversation with a curt 'Pronto!' and turned back to me.

'I'm very sorry, Mr Drummond,' he said awkwardly. 'But I can spare you no more time. Ah – that was one of my assistants. There is a new and very violent solar flare beginning, and my presence is required at the main telescope.'

Rising, he extended his hand across the desk. I shook it obediently and took my leave.

All the way back to Quito I kept wondering why he'd lied to me. From the half-dozen words I'd managed to catch, it had been perfectly definite that the call came not from anywhere within the observatory precincts, but from the main spaceport.

My head was buzzing with a horde of contradictory ideas. I struggled to sort them into logical patterns, but it was like sifting through three jigsaw puzzles mixed up together. I sat for a long while in the bar of my hotel hoping that a few margaritas would help, but they didn't. I got no further than the stage I'd reached in Acosta's office: the conclusion that stray energies running ahead of *Starventure* could account for the activity of the Sun, and that this in turn could explain the various news items Sandler had sent me, particularly the radio blackout and the aurorae – among which presumably, one must count the so-called monster in the sky.

So, then: what form would the energy take? Would there have been a burst of visible light? Conceivably. But it was too much to hope that one of the observatories here or on the Moon would have had a telescope pointing in the right direction to catch it.

There might, though, have been a brief shower of cosmic rays, and that would have shown up on someone's detectors, either in space or at one of the mountain monitoring stations. Assuming, of course, Earth had been in the path of the rays. I thought of calling the High Andes station to inquire, but then I remembered that they only culled their records at thirty-day intervals and wouldn't yet be able to give me an answer.

Continuing: if there had been any radiation at all, there would almost beyond doubt have been neutrinos in quantity. Hmm! What would be the effect if a sizable neutrino flux struck the Sun? I could only guess, but the guess suggested it would be rather dangerous to point a returning starship at it, or even at Earth.

Could that have been what so upset Acosta — news that the interior of the Sun had in fact been disturbed by the ship's return? I considered the possibility for some while and eventually dismissed it. If that were the case, he'd have been one of the people who first found out, not needed to be told by a caller from the spaceport.

Thinking of the spaceport . . .

I went in search of a phone on the slim chance that I might be able to contact one of my many acquaintances on the port staff, but after several minutes' fruitless trying I wound up with the answer I'd expected in the first place: all the phones were tied up with important traffic. I didn't really have the nerve to dispute the assertion.

Anyway, by now it was time to find my way to Carmen's place.

I got there seven minutes late, in accordance with her instructions, and that was exactly right. Carmen was exactly right too — she was wearing crimson, a colour I detest on women who can't carry it off like her. I admired her, I admired her new apartment, I admired her cooking and choice of wines. It was all set to be a hell of a fine evening. She seemed to have forgotten the unease she had felt earlier about her vision of Hermanos.

We were just finishing off with coffee and a fiery local cognac, and thinking about turning down the lights and playing some music, when there was a sound of shouting from outside. At first we ignored it. Then it grew — grew like a rising tide. When it was loud, we stopped talking and listened. When it was like a whole city crying out, we stared at each other and decided simultaneously to go out on the balcony.

The instant we opened the windows, we saw the light it was shedding — unearthly blue-green light, somehow sickly. We looked out, looked up. I felt Carmen's hand close suddenly and painfully on my wrist.

It was a monster in the sky.

I had been staring at in in total disbelief for a good half minute before I thought of recording it. I managed to break Carmen's grip on my wrist — she was just frozen, gazing upward with her mouth a little open and her eyes as wide as they would go. I tugged the recorder out of my pocket, turned the master switch from voice to vision recording, and began to scan. My hand was shaking so badly I wasn't sure it was worth the trouble; anyway, the damned thing filled so much of the sky I could barely fit it all in even with the lens at its widest setting.

Maybe the thing those Chilean fisherfolk had seen overhead was an auroral phenomenon. *This* wasn't.

We were on top floor of an eight-storey building. Opposite, across a wide avenue, was another building similar except that it had three more storeys and a huge lush roof garden where tall palms grew. Behind the trees was the monster's body. Its legs would be below the skyline, if it had legs. Sprawling up from there came hideously ridged folds of unhealthy blue, dim, like the phosphorescence of putrid fish. A mouth opened greeny-black, forty-five degrees above the horizon, and seemed enormous enough to gulp down our petty planet in a single devouring swallow. Within the mouth things writhed and dripped. And on either side of that tremendous opening there were eyes.

I say eyes, not knowing what else to call them. They were like blobs of blue-green quicksilver running around in black orbital pits, movement of coloured light over their surface giving the impression that they were round and rolling as though on the inner curvature of a bowl. If one of the blobs switched to the upper half of its black pit, so did the other in perfect unison; it was this which convinced me they were eyes.

Even through the viewfinder of the recorder, I felt that this was really a monstrous animal looking Earth over as though to decide where first it should sink its teeth.

And then it began to fade.

The shouting and screaming in the city faded with it, and I realized for the first time that there were people on other balconies all along the street, and in the roof garden across the way from us, staring up at the sky and uttering groaning prayers. Traffic in the road, as far as I could see in both directions, had stopped. People were clambering on the roofs of cars for a better view.

I kept on recording till the last smear of blue-green was gone, and the same familiar stars which the monster had obscured shone reassuringly down. Then I lowered the recorder and discovered that I had cramps from holding it still. I was also, for the first time in my life, literally soaked with sweat. I'd often been clammy from heat or tension, but now I could hardly have been wetter if I'd walked an hour in falling rain.

I moved my arms up and down, feeling the agony of cramp yield to the agony of returning circulation. Sure that Carmen would have retained her self-possession even in face of what had just happened, I contrived to make my first remark flippant. I said, 'Talk about signs and portents! Halley's Comet was nothing compared to that!'

She turned blindly to me, threw her arms around me, and burst into tears. As I'd told her this morning, she was always astonishing.

After I'd soothed her for a minute or so, she recovered and drew away from me. 'I'm sorry,' she muttered, stroking a tear from each eye with swift dabbing gestures. 'But . . . David, I did not tell you the whole truth when we had lunch. I am more than worried. I am frightened, and that — what we saw — broke me down.'

'It would break anybody,' I said. 'What in hell do you imagine it was?'

Giving another fearful glance at the sky — finding it clear and starry and normal — she fumbled out a cigarette from a nearby box. I had to light it for her, her hands were trembling so.

'I — I thought, you see,' she went on, 'when I saw Hermanos this morning, it must be what I have always been told about. I thought: yes, I must have the power my grandmother talks about.' She sounded more like herself now; I relaxed a trifle.

'But it proved that you had had a vision too, and now it seems — so have all the people in Quito! It must have been a vision, no? It can't have been real?'

For me, a vision capable of being seen by thousands of people must *ipso facto* possess reality. But I restricted my answer to a shrug, feeling my sweat-damp shirt move stickily on my back.

'What can it mean?' she cried suddenly. 'What can it mean?'

'I don't know. But I've just realized we can find out whether it was a mass hallucination or whether there was something actually up there.' I hefted my recorder in my hand and strode across to the phone on the other side of the room. I wasn't sure that phones in Quito had recorder-playback attachments, and half expected to have to peel the insulation off the cables, but as it turned out this was an up-to-date model with full accessory equipment. I clipped the recorder to the vision strand of the cable and set it to replay.

In the half-second that followed, I hoped desperately that it *had* been a mass hallucination, and that the screen would show I had recorded only the buildings and the sky. But I had the monster — mouth, eyes and all. Three full minutes of it had gone down on the crystals.

I looked around at Carmen when it was over. She was staring at the now blank screen as fixedly as she had stared at the thing in the sky. Alarmed, I spoke her name.

She gave a forced laugh and reached to drop her forgotten cigarette in the ashtray. She said, 'Thank you, David, I'm all right. But — but *does* this mean the thing was real?'

'It means,' I said, choosing my words with care, 'that there really was a pattern of lights in the sky. We didn't imagine that. But as to the pattern corresponding to a solid substantial monster — no, that's out of the question.'

'Just as impossible as it was for me to see Hermanos today, or you to see your brother?' Carmen spoke in a tone I remembered. I knew better than to contradict outright, so I just put on a sceptical expression. It didn't last.

There was a pause. At length she said, 'David, do you think many people would have had the presence of mind to take pictures?'

'Probably,' I said, though I rather thought not. The thing could only have lasted six or seven minutes altogether, and in spite of having my recorder in my pocket I'd practically forgotten to record it myself.

'But it would be worth it for you to send the pictures to your press agency?' Receiving my nod she went on, 'Then why don't you?'

I hesitated. 'It will be very expensive on your phone bill if I do it from here,' I said finally. 'Shall I go find a pay phone where I can use my credit card?'

'No!' she said with sudden violence, and came over to me, laying one small hand on mine as though to reassure herself of my reality. 'No, David. You must not leave me — not for a minute. Tonight I am too afraid to be alone.'

5

Three or four times that night she cried out in her sleep, woke herself up far enough to feel my arms around her, and as it were drew them tight like armour on her smooth supple body. My sleep was shallow, too, and stained with nightmare.

Not long after it was light, a little past six o'clock, we woke together and found it impossible to sleep again. We lay for a while in silence, each knowing that the other too was wondering whether the monster in the sky could have been no more than the figment of an evil dream. But the world was real, the clutch of hand on hand, the brush of leg against leg, the acutely perceived wrinkling of the bedsheets which our restless slumber had crumpled and folded across the mattress. Each shift in search of comfort rendered escape more impossible.

At length, as though she could read my thoughts through my skin, Carmen said without looking at me, 'David, I feel that you want to go away.'

For once, she was a trifle less than perfectly correct. I wanted most of all to stay; this woman of fire and ice was a source of reassurance and security in a world suddenly become intolerably random. But I *needed* to leave. I needed to go out and find why the universe was different from yesterday — if there was anyone who could inform me.

So I said, 'No, I don't want to. I think I must.'

She reeled from the bed and stood up, stretching to the tips of her fingers. Around a yawn she said, 'Then I shall have to let you. But only on condition that you at once tell me whatever you learn about last night.'

I made the promise, and went into the clear warm morning.

The monster had not been a nightmare. There were screaming headlines about it on the early newspaper bills. Many of the citizens of Quito had spent the night in churches and cathedrals, praying; now they were coming out, hundreds at a time, looking nervously skyward after every step as they went to buy newspapers or hear radio news bulletins in bars and cafés, wishing to disbelieve their own memories and finding it impossible.

I kept thinking of the Chilean fisherfolk seeing what I had glibly dismissed as an aurora.

Last night, rather than drive to Carmen's, I'd taken a cab from my hotel and had to return by the same means. The driver of the cab I found now was scared, and made me frightened too because he was driving with his eyes more on the sky than on the road. Most other drivers seemed to be doing the same. St Christopher, whose medal hung on the dashboard, must have been working overtime. The man asked me one question as I got into the back seat: 'Did you see it?'

I said yes.

'So did I,' he muttered and fell moodily silent until we reached my hotel.

It was too early for the morning's mail, and anyway I wasn't expecting anything — barring Solar Press, no one had an address for me more recent than a hotel in Caracas. But there was a message for me at the reception desk in the lobby; I was to call a certain Captain Brandt, who had been trying to contact me all yesterday afternoon, at a number which began with the same local code as the spaceport.

I wasn't going to talk to strangers on an empty stomach, I decided. I tucked the note in my pocket and went to have breakfast in company of the papers and the stack of material Sandler had 'faxed to me, cudgeling my brains to determine whether there really could be a connection between all these snippets and the return of the starship, as I'd suggested to Acosta.

My brain had been sluggish since waking, that was obvious; a few cups of strong Colombian coffee set that right, and I abruptly realized, in the middle of biting a slice of toast, that I had a prize in my pocket. I gulped down what was in my mouth and abandoned the table in search of a phone.

This early in the day, I wasn't certain of being able to reach anyone at the local office of Prensam — Solar Press's associate in most countries south of Mexico — but I was in luck. My old and good friend Manuel Segura was there, and had — as he told me when he'd finished wasting time on greetings — been there all night. One of the things he was looking for was some decent colour coverage of the monster; so far he hadn't even found a still colour picture and was having to make do with a batch of blurred black-and-whites taken by one of the local people. When I said I had three minutes of usable colour, he practically climbed down the phone cable to get at me, and then calmed sufficiently to record a verbal agreement in respect of Latin American rights for thirty seconds of it. I had sold only a North American exclusive to Solar Press last night, with first-run Eurasian rights as a bonus, and it struck me as good sense to dispose of what additional rights I could before they came after me with a request for the whole lot.

Then we got round to other aspects of what had happened. Manuel had access to much more than what had been in the papers I'd read with breakfast, of course — he'd seen everything that came off the beams at the Prensam office and had also had several eye-witness accounts which he digested for me. None of them differed much from what I'd seen, however. Both government and church had appealed for calm, but so far people seemed more puzzled than hysterical. The monster had been reported from as far away as Lima, and he suspected that not all the sightings had yet been listed.

I referred him to the Chilean episode of the day before yesterday, and he checked back because he hadn't heard about it. It turned out that his agency had carried the story for only a few hours before it was ousted by a strike in Bogota and a landslide on the outskirts of Rio. Cursing the shortsightedness of the person responsible, he declared he was going to resurrect it.

Not, I thought privately, that anyone would be much the wiser . . .

When I was through talking to Manuel, I called the number I'd been given by the reception clerk. As I'd anticipated, I found myself being answered from the switchboard at the starship base, and the extension I was put through to proved to belong to a fresh-faced young officer of the UN Space Force.

'Ah, Mr Drummond!' he exclaimed. 'I'm so glad to make your acquaintance — I've been an admirer of your writing for many years! My name's Brandt, of course, assistant chief of personnel.'

I nodded and waited for him to explain why he'd been so eager to get in touch.

'Part of my job is to notify the relatives of *Starventure's* crew about the arrangements for the landing. Not a very easy task, I'm afraid, because right now everything's so vague. We don't even have a date for their Earthfall, let alone any idea how long it will take to process them through debriefing and quarantine and so on. But when the press department told me you were right here in Quito I thought I'd call you anyway, because as I say I really do enjoy your work very much. By the way, I hear you were first with the news again!'

I said grumpily, 'Sheer chance.'

He smiled conspiratorially, as though certain he had seen through my modest disclaimer of super-reportorial sixth sense. 'Well, that's as it may be. But what I really wanted to say was that — ah — well, naturally having a brother in the crew will entitle you to all the facilities for family contact we can offer after the landing, and you can be assured that your professional status won't make the least bit of difference. To us, I mean. I imagine it may not be quite the same among your colleagues!'

There and then I decided I didn't like Brandt. I couldn't recollect that at the time of the launching anyone had needed to excuse me for being Leon's brother, nor that any of my fellow reporters had regarded the relationship as giving me unfair advantages. I cut short what he had gone on to say — something about looking forward to meeting me in person as soon as things were a bit quieter at the base — and the moment his image faded from the screen was annoyed with myself. Likeable or not, Brandt might well have been offended by my curtness, and I was obviously going to need all the help I could get from people in positions of influence.

Still, it was done now. I sighed, wondering whether before I left the phonebooth I ought to make any more calls, and realized that by this time Professor Acosta might well be available at the observatory. Before *Starventure* entered orbit this city was bound to be crawling with top scientific talent, but right now Acosta was about as top as came handy. I called the outside number of the observatory.

33

Busy line. I wasn't at all surprised. I stayed patiently at the phone, calling one time after another, for a good five minutes before I hit a break in the flow and a harassed switchboard operator answered on a voice-only circuit.

I identified myself and asked to speak to Acosta, and she told me sharply that he was far too busy to talk to anybody. Before she could cut the connection, though, I quoted to her what Acosta had said the previous afternoon about being happier to make an exception for me than for most other people, and persuaded her to remind him of his own words. Then I waited.

Eventually Acosta's face appeared on the screen, with a fixed expression of annoyance; his voice, however, was reasonably level as he addressed me.

'Good morning, Mr Drummond. I'm sure you're going to ask what I think of the strange apparition in the sky last night.'

'I am indeed,' I said. 'Can you −?'

I got no further. He leaned towards the phone just in time for the picture-melt to catch him and spoke with passionate emphasis.

'*No*, Mr Drummond! I saw this thing in the sky last night. All my preconceptions − all my common sense − told me, "It's impossible!" Yet I recall that I saw it. There was a picture in my morning paper to show it was no mere hallucination. Yesterday I was a sober scientist. Today I feel like an ignorant child. Because there is no room in my science for monsters in the heavens! Yesterday I could agree with you that those fishermen in Chile were naïve, and mistook the Aurora Australis for an enormous face. Today I will keep my mouth shut. Sorry, Mr Drummond. But − *goodbye*.'

The screen blanked. I was still staring at it in dismay when the hotel's own operator cut in to tell me there was an outside call for me; I agreed to take it, and Carmen appeared. She looked and sounded even more troubled than Acosta.

'David, you are Leon's only close relative, no?' she said without preamble.

'Yes, of course I am. Why?'

'I called my home, and everyone was joyful about the ship returning. But my father said that my nephew Hermanos − the one who is six years old and was named after

34

my brother because he was born the same day of the year — little Hermanos came home from school yesterday and said he had seen his namesake-uncle on his way there in the morning. They are all saying it is a good omen, that it means he is safe, except my grandmother who says it shows he is in danger. David, what am I to think?'

'I was just talking to Professor Acosta,' I said after a brief pause. 'His view is that it's best to try not to think about it at all at the moment, and I guess I'm inclined to agree with him.'

'You have learned nothing new, then?'

'Nothing of any importance. I spoke to my friend Manuel Segura at Prensam, and to someone at the starship base I took an immediate dislike to, but right now my brain feels numb and I can barely dream up the right kind of questions. I do intend to call New York, though, and I guess I'll probably drop in to see Chambord at the UN press office. Ah . . . Suppose I meet you for lunch again, same place as yesterday?'

'Yes. Yes, please, David. But earlier than yesterday. A half hour earlier.'

Sandler looked haggard. He paid me an absent-minded compliment about getting such a good-quality recording of the monster in the sky, and then demanded to know whether I'd drawn any conclusions from the material he'd sent me.

I told him no, which wasn't more than half a lie, and said that furthermore I still hadn't fathomed the connection he himself must have seen between the ill-assorted items.

'It's hard to describe,' he sighed. 'It wasn't thinking so much as feeling. There comes a time when coincidences — say, do you cook?'

I knew cookery was a hobby of his; to me it's something you hire to have done. I said, 'Not any more often than I can help. Why?'

'Never made a white sauce? It's mainly milk, butter, flour. You stir it over the heat and the flour cooks. There comes a moment when it's cooked though, and instead of flour and milk you have a blended sauce. You can't see the change — you feel it through the way your spoon moves. Well, I got that same kind of impression from the bunch of stories I picked on. I worked two or three of my staff half to death over them; then I had the bright idea of asking you to scratch the itch for me.'

'You sound as though it's still bothering you,' I said.

'I'm afraid it is. I don't suppose you've had any time to follow the matter up, have you?'

I gave him a bald summary of what Acosta had told me yesterday, and he grunted.

'Pretty much what scientists up here have been saying — those that believe something has actually happened, like an unexpected effect of the starship's re-entry. But most of the people I've tried to talk to have shrugged me off: *Starventure* is back and I'm busy.'

He became brisk. 'Well, was there anything else?'

'Just one point. Are you sending anyone down here from Solar to cover the landing?'

'Are we not!' He snorted. 'Granted, you're an ace in the hole and worth your weight in uranium, but should we risk you falling down a mountain? Kaye Green, Brian Watchett and Don Hapgood will be in Quito this afternoon; they have your hotel address and will get in touch when they arrive. If you chance across anything — anything at all — which you don't have time to follow up yourself, let them have it, won't you? Don't forget you're on a ten thousand per week retainer as of yesterday, and we'd like something to show for the investment.'

'You'll get it,' I said. 'If it's there to be had.'

I cut the connection thoughtfully. Kaye, Brian and Don, all old friends of mine, were *the* top trio on the Solar Press staff. Aside from the purely scientific angle, I was going to be a fifth wheel when they showed up — and of course, aside from having a brother in the crew, I amended with a scowl due to remembering Brandt's earlier remark.

That state of affairs would suit me fine; I was out of the habit of meeting twice-daily deadlines.

I dropped by at the UN office on the way to my lunch date and found — as I'd expected — that the foyer was full of hopeful cubs camping out on the benches, some asleep, some trying to sleep, some trying to stay awake. They'd probably been here all night.

Well, they'd learn. Henri Chambord was as good a PR man as you could find and scrupulously honest about his news releases. I'd got a beat by turning up in his office yesterday, but if I'd gone down on bended knee and begged him to delay preparation of the full release, he'd have spat in my face and withdrawn my press pass.

I didn't get in to see him this morning; Ramona told me he was tied up in a conference, planning interview facilities with the crew when they were checked out of quarantine. It made sense to have everything ready to roll beforehand, even though no date could yet be fixed for the end of their quarantine, because the lowest odds any expert had ever quoted me against the risk of Centauran bacteria surviving in a human body were a million to one, and the chances were that they'd be able to undergo their full-scale debriefing right here on Earth . . . where naturally every reporter in the hemisphere would want to get at them.

Accordingly I contented myself with picking up the morning poopsheet. From it I learned that the tugs were matching velocities with *Starventure*, that the ship was still transmitting code-groups only but that when the range shortened enough there was going to be a planet-wide broadcast of personal messages from everyone aboard, and that everything was proceeding normally.

I didn't even bother to take the sheet with me. I balled it up and dropped it in the wastebasket beside Ramona's desk, apologizing for the scare I'd given her yesterday when I stormed in. She smiled charmingly and giggled not so charmingly and I went to lunch with Carmen.

6

I had many things in mind to say to her when we took our places opposite each other at the table. But, unexpectedly, there followed a long period of silence: on her part, because she was preoccupied, and on mine because, on glancing towards her, I felt as though I was seeing her for the first time. When I did find words to utter, they came of their own accord.

'I've been thinking that I know you pretty well because I met you more than two years ago,' I said. 'But I've seen you – what? – on not more than fifty days out of seven

37

hundred plus. And I just realized that I don't know you at all, because I never saw you so serious as you are now.'

She didn't answer.

'It suits you,' I said, fumbling for the reason why and suddenly getting it. 'It exalts you, that's the word. I can see a volcano of personality behind your face — the glow which always flickers there and makes men look at you twice without knowing why. But today it's turned on full, and . . . my God, you're almost terrifying!'

I folded my nails hard into my palms to stop my hands from shaking. She had a presence like a stormcloud.

A smile lit the cloud and seemed to show me the whole world as lightning whipcracks darkness away from a landscape.

'Dear David,' she said. 'Do you know why I'm so serious? It's because I'm afraid of going mad. If it were not for you being so sane and balanced, and yet having the same thing happen to you, I'd be unable to think clearly at all.'

'Is it what happened to your nephew that frightens you?'

'His tale of having seen my brother? No. I accept the reality of second sight, as I told you yesterday.'

'But he's only a little boy,' I objected. 'I think you said he's six. It's more likely to be imagination than second sight.'

'Many children are said to have the power. It was children who last saw the fairies; it was the innocence of children which turned them from cruel, capricious creatures into beings as harmless and pretty as butterflies.'

'Children aren't all that innocent,' I said. 'They can be heartlessly savage.'

'Children who are sincerely loved are innocent,' Carmen insisted. 'If they're cruel, it's to revenge on weaker creatures wrongs done to them by stronger ones. But I didn't want to talk about children.' She bowed her head, wide eyes gazing at but not seeing the spotless white table top before her. 'I want — I need — to talk about my own fears.'

I took my time over devising a reply. At length I said, 'I don't see you have any reason to be afraid of mental breakdown. The world itself seems to have gone crazy, but I never met anyone in my life tougher than you. You'd bend and spring right back where the average person would snap apart.'

'But the monster in the sky —'

'All Quito saw that!' I cut in. 'It was seen at least as far away as Lima! Acosta saw it, a sober scientist with an international reputation. The man who drove me back to my hotel this morning saw it. Everyone saw it — just go and ask around!'

'No, you don't understand!' she exclaimed passionately. 'What I fear is to find that I *imagined* all Quito seeing it, and you as well. Sometimes the power — like boiling water poured into a cold glass — can shatter the mind.' She leaned forward and laid an imploring hand on top of mine. 'What is happening, David? You understand about science. Is there any straightforward explanation?'

'It seems possible that it's something to do with *Starventure's* return to normal space,' I said slowly.

'That tells me nothing. How can one judge whether the monsters might not have appeared at some other time? The one in the sky over Chile was seen before the ship returned; your former boss in New York compiled his list of strange events before he knew the ship was back, and if you hadn't come by chance to Quito you'd have heard from him before you walked into the press office here. Would you have said the same then?'

Almost embarrassed at my inability to offer the reassurance she craved, I could only shrug. 'Right now,' I confessed, 'I've run out of ideas. I can only wait and try to get in touch with people who know more than I do.'

'Then do me a favour, David. I told you I'd like to find out whether anyone else who has a relative aboard *Starventure* had a vision like yours and mine. Make some inquiries and tell me. I think you'll find the answer is yes. What it will mean if it is, I don't know. But it will be another fact, and we have so desperately few.'

The Solar Press team arrived as Sandler had promised, in the middle of the afternoon. They called my hotel from the airport, and I arranged to meet them at the UN press office. Chambord was in conference again but had promised another release at six o'clock, so to use up the time I took them to a nearby bar and gave them a rundown on the situation.

Don Hapgood specialized in the transcription of recorded material; it had been said of him that he could put

39

on a printed page everything including a tone of voice. Kaye Green, a bony redhead with a walk like a horse, was usually employed on rewrite work, where her talent for cramming gut-wrenching emotion into prosaic facts showed to best advantage. Only the biggest stories drew her from her New York desk, but this one of course was a giant. As for Brian Watchett, he knew *everybody*; he had contacts on all continents and at least some of the other planets and could always be relied on to find his way to the man who knew the inside story. Short of coming to Quito himself, Sandler could hardly have put Solar Press in a stronger position.

Over beers, I told them about my own involvement to date. When I came to the appearance of the monster in the sky, they demanded to see the complete recording, so since I still had the crystals on me we adjourned to a pay phonebooth and stuffed ourselves in while I played it over. We could scarcely breathe, but that was no great drawback — for the three minutes the job took we either didn't want to breathe or simply forgot. The replay was almost worse than the original event. It was a reminder in broad daylight of what reason yearned to dismiss as a bad dream.

We returned quietly and soberly to our table. It was some while before Brian broke the silence, fixing me with his sharp brown eyes half buried in the rolls of fat which testified to his love of good living.

'David, there's a rumour going around that all this has a connection with a re-entry of *Starventure*. Does that make scientific sense, or is it a wild guess of Hank Sandler's?'

'I figure it will be another couple of days before I can give you an authoritative answer,' I said. 'When the top talent has arrived and had a chance to settle in, I'll be able to ask the people whose word I'm most inclined to take. Until the ship's in Earth-orbit, though, everyone will be too busy or too excited.'

'Your brother worked on the stardrive,' Don said. 'Some of it must have rubbed off. How about giving us your own answer to be going on with?'

'All right,' I sighed. 'My opinion is — yes, there probably is a link with the ship's return. As you must know, during the operation of the drive *Starventure* ceases to exist in our normal universe, but the crew remain aware — their hearts beat, their clocks continue to tick away time. Any relati-

40

vistic effects observable at the moment of switching on the drive . . . hell, it gets abstruse at that point, and anyway it's irrelevant. What matters is that in our universe only the potential of *Starventure* continues to exist, and as it were trickles to a point nearer Alpha Centauri, but subjectively a "real" ship and a "real" crew must go on existing because that's what comes out again at the destination. The problem is —'

'Where?' suggested Brian softly.

'Exactly. For convenience, because "existence" implies some kind of space to exist *in*, we invented the name hyperspace and defined it as non-Einsteinian. But this is only sticking on labels. My guess is that the label "hyperspace" has a real referent, and that hyperphotonic velocity is also real, so that when the ship slows to re-enter normal space you may get a surging front of — of ripples in the continuum, with accompanying energies, like Cherenkov radiation.'

I'd always been glad I took up science reporting after they started to teach Einsteinian rather than Newtonian principles in schools. Even Kaye seemed to be following me, though she was woefully unscientific because she was in a line of business dependent on thick-clotted emotion and for her, rational logic was sometimes an actual handicap.

But it was that which carried her over a jump that no one else I knew had yet attempted. She said, 'Did *Starventure* bring something back from this other universe she's been travelling in?'

An automatically contemptuous retort died on my lips as I realized I'd been subconsciously wondering the same thing. I still hadn't replied when Brian grunted and spoke up.

'They ran a robot ship all around the solar system first,' he pointed out. 'And I don't recall hearing that anything like this happened as a result.'

The cases weren't comparable, and I said so. 'For one thing, the robot ship was tiny compared to *Starventure* — barely big enough for one man to ride. Statistical uncertainty prevents us from moving large masses over short distances with any accuracy. In fact Alpha Centauri is barely far enough away to offer a convenient journey for a ship of *Starventure's* size. Paradoxically, it would have been

41

easier to go about twenty-five light-years.'

'Some kind of exponential relationship?' frowned Don, keeping up manfully.

'I have a note of it somewhere,' I said, nodding. 'All the indices are irrationals, and there are lots of them.'

At that point Kaye made it obvious that she hadn't heard a word since she last spoke up, for she said to the air, 'Things from another universe! My God, what a story!'

'Don't write it,' I said. 'In heaven's name! Isn't one universe enough for you to be going on with?'

For a short answer: no. Oh, there was plenty of excitement on the surface. Quito was coming to a boil. The airport, the streets, the rail terminal, the hotels, all crammed to bursting-point as the visitors poured in — reporters, sensation-seekers, the crew's relatives, scientists, UN high brass — creating masses of minor detail for Don to tape, Kaye to edit and cable to New York. Optimistic city officials ordered the municipal banners hung out in the streets as they had been for *Starventure's* departure. Prices doubled.

In the midst of all this, Carmen had to maintain her usual daily round of work, friends and family. It wasn't so bad for me; I could find moments to close my eyes and picture Leon to myself and think a burning question: *Leon, has it changed you to go among the stars? Are we still good friends as well as brothers?*

But Carmen's face showed a distant pain.

It made me feel dreadfully guilty when, every time she begged me for information, I had to say that I'd learned nothing. I had no alternative, though, because that was the simple ugly truth. Somewhere someone had built a wall.

And it wasn't someone who'd taken offence at me personally, either, who had clamped down on the supply of solid factual news. Virtually every science correspondent and science writer on Earth had converged on Quito by now, and all day long I was being greeted by old acquaintances in twenty different versions of highly accented English. When I pinned my colleagues down long enough to compare notes, their experience confirmed mine.

Not since ancient Athens had such a dazzling display of intellect assembled in a single city. Every Nobel Prize winner in science for the last decade had flown in. Could I get to talk to any of them? Not on the bottom of the Pacific. I met people I was anxious to interview walking down the street or waiting on corners looking for cabs; I said, 'Professor, I'm David Drummond. I wonder if —' And I got a headshake on the instant. On the phone, the answer was stereotyped almost to the point of being a cliché: 'He's in conference right now, at the starship base. Suppose you try again tomorrow?'

There was no hope of getting into the spaceport itself. I'd tried, but their security was unbelievable. Oh, maybe if I'd tried a little harder . . . Yet somehow I couldn't bring myself to that point, not only because of the risk of my future career if I got caught sneaking through one of their fences, but because the people there were genuinely very damned busy. Once or twice a day at least there were takeoffs and landings, with rather more of the former than the latter, and knowing how complicated it still was to launch a ship into orbit I had to admit they must be working under phenomenal pressure to keep up such a schedule. I watched a couple of the takeoffs through my high-power binoculars, sitting on a nearby mountain and wondering why so many scientific notables should be spending so *long* in conference down there. No matter how hard I hauled on the grapevine, I couldn't find an answer.

The same evening we first saw *Starventure* again with the naked eye, glittering in the light of the exhausts of the rocket-driven tugs gentling her into orbit on the night side of Earth, a blue-dripping monster with claws as big as itself appeared over a rock called Santadonna Island in the South Pacific.

On the island was a satellite tracking station, and the staff there recorded so many data that although by now monsters were coming thick and fast, this one became a standard of reference. It spanned forty degrees of sky from tip to tip, moving irregularly like a spastic crab. Its brightness was not much higher than that of the Milky Way, and the patches of its body which seemed black proved to be radiating in the ultraviolet.

And its mass, apparently, was *nil*. For the sake of calculation someone assumed that it had a density close to that of protoplasm (which was absurd anyway; protoplasm on that scale would imply a paper-thin amoeba) and worked out that at the limits of the atmosphere it ought to have noticeable gravitational effects. None were recorded. Moreover, it had no detectable orbital velocity. Consequently it ought to have come crashing down like the Arizona Meteorite. It stayed right where it was until it began to fade.

On the increasingly rare occasions when I did see Quito's famous scientific visitors coming from or going to the starship base, they looked uniformly depressed. Grimly, I wondered if it was the weighing and measuring of the Santadonna monster which had affected them — because weighing and measuring lent an air of authenticity to the reports — or whether it was something else. Something directly to do with *Starventure*.

Maybe to do with Leon.

Hell and damnation, what was shutting their mouths?

7

I respected — more, I trusted — Henri Chambord. I was certain he was doing his job as efficiently and as . . . well, as *kindly* as he was permitted to. But he was giving out information drop by drop, and over the next few days it turned into a kind of Chinese water torture.

Drip: Alpha Centauri has planets, but none of them are habitable by man.

Next day — drip: experts have gone up to *Starventure's* orbit, to examine the crew for possible infection. They landed on two planets and fourteen moons and asteroids.

The day after — drip: personal messages from the crewmen to their families. Mine was very short, but that was typical of Leon and therefore reassuring. When Leon was about fourteen or so he used to accuse me of being a Big Brother in the Orwellian sense as well as literally, having just read *1984* as background to a school history class. So it was appropriate for his message to run: 'Don't look now, but I think Big Brother is watching us.'

It wasn't until an hour or two after I first read it that I

started wondering whether by 'Big Brother' he meant the creatures in the sky . . .

But there was no way of finding out whether that absurd-seeming suspicion was justified. Hammer as I might on the intangible barriers surrounding the spacecraft, I received what my colleagues did: today a drip, the next day another. No pictures of the crew. No film of the Centaurian planets. No interviews by radio, even on a voice-only circuit.

Little by little I grew aware that I was horribly afraid.

On the evening of the seventh day after the return Brian Watchett walked into my hotel's dining room just as Carmen and I were taking our places for dinner. I hadn't seen him in two days, but that wasn't surprising. There were other important people currently in Quito than the scientists, and he was probably better able to get the politicians to open their mouths.

Looking very upset, he marched up to our table without ceremony. 'David! I've got to have a word with you,' he muttered with a sidelong glance at Carmen. I introduced him to her, and she gave a nod.

'Is it something about — up there?' she demanded.

'Yes,' Brian said.

'Then perhaps you'd like me to leave you, David?' She made to rise, but I put out my hand to stop her.

'Carmen also has a brother aboard *Starventure*,' I told Brian. 'Anything you say to me, I think she's entitled to hear as well, and if you don't want it to go any further, you only need to ask.'

He hesitated, but agreed. I had the waiter show us to a larger table in a more secluded corner of the room, and the moment he had taken our orders Brian plunged ahead.

'David, something must have gone extremely wrong with *Starventure*.'

Carmen put her hand to her mouth. I pressed my knee against hers under the table and answered in a level voice.

'I've been suspecting as much. But what makes you so sure?'

'Did you know that the Chairman of the General Assembly is in Quito? Or that the Secretary-General was here yesterday and left again this morning? Of course you didn't. Practically no one was told. Can you think of any other reason for keeping the movements of top UN officials a secret, other than a ghastly emergency? And can you think of any other reason why old friends of mine should have called off appointments they'd made with me on the orders of the UN staff at the spaceport?'

'Orders? Are you sure?'

'I wasn't at first — I took my friends' word that they'd been delayed by unexpected commitments. But in the end I bribed a few hotel clerks, and there's no room for doubt. They were lying. They were actually warned off talking to the press.'

I glanced at Carmen. Her face was pale as death. I said, 'I've had the same kind of trouble. Most of the major scientists who've come here are personal friends of mine; they'll normally talk to me even if they insist on it being off the record. This time I can't even get a civil hello out of them.'

There was a growling sound in the distance, and people stopped talking for a moment to listen to it. I did the same. When it died away, I jerked my head in the direction of the spaceport.

'Another thing. I've been counting takeoffs and landings at the port. They've made enough trips to bring down the entire crew and all their records and geological specimens — anything the starship could have carried in her holds. That was another landing, the tenth since she was brought into orbit. Brian, what do you suggest we do?'

'We're going to have to blow it open,' he said matter-of-factly. 'Have you heard some of the rumours that are going around? I was talking to Hank Sandler a few minutes ago, and he chilled my blood. People are getting impatient, and the monsters are fraying their nerves. They're avenging angels sent to punish man for trespassing in heaven — or, a bit more scientifically, they're creatures from Centaurus looking us over while they get ready to invade. Hank said he'd been approached by the high brass and asked to put out a denial of any connection between the monsters and the ship!' He added the last comment in a tone that suggested he'd been personally affronted.

'I suppose he told them what they could do with the idea?'

'Of course. Practically threw them out of his office. He was still fuming when I spoke to him, though. Said he wasn't a hired liar, he was an honest reporter, and if the public didn't get some solid facts to satisfy them after the big buildup, there was bound to be trouble. In fact, he told me to get together with you and see what we could do to improve the situation.'

'Such as?'

'I was hoping you'd tell me that,' Brian countered wryly. 'Perhaps we could go and challenge Chambord.'

'Henri wouldn't play,' I said. 'I've known him long enough to be sure of that.'

'Then how about this man Brandt, the assistant chief of personnel? He strikes me as a weak point in their organization — all surface and no substance. Or if we must we can go right to General Cassiano, so long as we talk to someone who takes us seriously. Hank says, and I agree with him, that we've got to issue a warning. We've got to say that unless we're immediately given convincing reasons to the contrary tomorrow morning we're going to publish our grounds for believing that important facts are being kept from the public. We've got to force the truth out into the open, David. If there has been a disaster, delaying the announcement will only make matters worse by allowing these rumours to outstrip the truth.'

I pushed back my chair. I had suddenly realized I was far too badly worried about Leon to waste time on something trivial like food.

Carmen came with us. Neither of us thought of telling her to stay behind, and she probably wouldn't have agreed anyway.

We did go to see Chambord first after all, because on reflection I felt it was only fair to let him know of our decision and — good pressman that he was — his reaction when he heard our ultimatum was a sigh of relief.

'Believe me, my friends,' he said, 'I'm not sorry you've decided on this course. I myself have pestered General Cassiano till I'm exhausted. I've pleaded to be told at least why I could have no more news — you understand, I've passed on every fact I've been given. But you must get inside the — the Maginot Line which surrounds the base. You must try someone like Captain Brandt. Put pressure on him. He's a weak man. He will cave in and let you through to higher authority, where anyone else at a similar level would adroitly set you running in circles.'

He hesitated. Then, rising to offer his hand to us, he concluded, 'And, if I might add a request for one small favour . . .? Whatever you are told, let me know as well, will you? Isn't it ironic that *I* have to ask *you* for information?'

Pleased that his estimate of Brandt squared with mine, I thanked him for his advice and good wishes, and we headed for the spaceport personnel department. This was located in a clump of ugly low concrete buildings which also included the main administrative offices for the port and barracks for the technical personnel, several miles away from the port proper, at which for fear of accidents there was only an irreducible minimum of accommodation. It took us some time to get anyone to rout Brandt out for us, but persistence and a lot of name-dropping managed it.

Appearing in a crumpled open-necked shirt, leisure pants and down-at-the-heel slippers, he reacted as Chambord had predicted. His first pretence of delight at having such distinguished visitors faded swiftly, and gave way to blustering about our abuse of press privileges. We wore that down, and he switched from prevarication to threats about having us forcibly thrown off the premises and denied access to any more UN-sponsored press conferences. Brian, who was a great deal better at handling recalcitrant bureaucrats than I was, silkily reminded him that even if he denied us press privileges our employers wouldn't, and asked if he wanted to see his name splashed all over the world's newspapers and TV screens as the man responsible for keeping information about the starship's crew from their families. At that point he started to scream at us, and that was what unexpectedly won us our victory.

He had received us in an office on the ground floor of a building which also contained bachelor quarters for senior staff not living in Quito with their wives. The walls were badly soundproofed; when Brandt raised his voice he could probably be heard three or four rooms away.

All at once the door of the office was thrown open and an angry man strode in. 'Brandt!' he snapped. 'I'm trying to get an hour's rest before I go back to the port! How can I when you're yelling like a madman?'

The newcomer was tall, thickset and brown-haired. On the shoulders of his olive-green UN uniform he wore two general's stars. He looked familiar, but I was still trying to place him when Brian rose to his feet.

'So sorry to have disturbed you, General Suvorov,' he said, and went on to summarize why we had come. I hardly heard him because I was so annoyed with myself for not immediately recognizing General Cassiano's second-in-command.

I glanced at Carmen's face. She was absolutely still and very white. I tried to give her a reassuring smile, but she didn't notice.

Suddenly Brian uttered my name, nudging me to pick up my cue. I did so, leaning back in my chair with Suvorov's hard eyes on me.

'I happen to be both a reporter and a brother to a member of the starship's crew,' I said. '*Starventure* has been in orbit for a week, and all I've heard from my brother is a message of a few words and a vague assurance that he's all right. I don't believe he's all right. I don't believe anything is all right. And if I don't get positive information tonight, I propose to tell the world what I think tomorrow.'

Suvorov gestured at Carmen, asking me a question with his eyebrows. 'Señorita Iglesias,' I said. 'You should recognize the name. She also has a brother among the crew.'

I could see tiredness driving a decision to the front of his mind; the instant he reached it, his expression altered from anger to grim determination. 'Very well,' he said heavily. 'You can have the facts. I warn you, we shan't permit you to publish the information . . . but your better judgment will confirm that it's wiser not to. Brandt, get me a car at once. The hell with my trying to rest — how can anyone rest at a time like this?'

Brandt gulped and snatched at his phone. He was a different person when a general was in the room. Suvorov looked briefly at Carmen again.

'I'm sorry for you, Miss Iglesias,' he said after a pause. 'We are all sorry for everyone.'

Puzzled, hesitant, and — speaking for myself — afraid of what we were going to learn, we went out to the car when it arrived. Suvorov told the driver to move over into the front passenger seat and took the wheel himself; Brian, Carmen and I got in behind. I could feel Carmen trembling when I put my arm around her shoulders.

Suvorov switched on all four headlights and the spots as well, spun the car almost in its own length, and sent us plunging down a beam of yellow-white light into the dark fastness of the mountains.

He was a terrifying driver. Although the spaceport was only fifteen miles distant, the road was twenty-five miles long, and clung crazily to the edge of precipices, twisting and writhing. Previously I'd only travelled it by day, and even then I'd thought I would rather not have travelled it at all. To ride with someone who treated it like a straight and level parkway was so alarming that I nearly brought back what little of my dinner I'd swallowed before Brian urged us away.

Other vehicles approached, and Suvorov hit a switch on the dash which flashed the car's lights in a coded rhythm. The oncoming drivers pulled to the side and we went swaying past without slowing. None of us said anything.

The road swooped down towards the starship base. Fierce arc lights bathed the three-mile-wide artificial plateau of the port, revealing two ferries on the ground, one being unloaded of some cargo, the other being fuelled for a return leap into the sky. At a barrier blocking the road, sentries signalled with flashlights, and Suvorov made the tyres cry out as he braked. He looked out of the window and shouted something I didn't catch; the sentries saluted and waved us by.

Just beyond the barrier, he parked the car and curtly told us to get out. We obeyed, and followed him around a narrow concrete path to an opening in the side of a vast rock — part of the mountains themselves, apparently. Huge soundproof and air-tight doors stood open, giving access to a wide corridor. There was a smell of electricity and a noise of machinery; the solid stone floor vibrated a trifle underfoot.

He led us for perhaps five minutes along the corridor, acknowledging salutes from junior personnel coming in the opposite direction with a mere sketched wave of his weary right arm, until at last he halted before a sliding door. He pressed a stud set into its surface and it squeaked aside.

Beyond was a low-ceilinged room where men and women with tense faces sat round a table stacked with large coloured photographs. There was a computer keyboard in the far corner. One woman was on her feet, as though she had been addressing her companions; both she and the rest of the group looked astonished and a little angry at the interruption.

'Sorry to break in on you,' Suvorov said brusquely. 'But I want to show these people a copy of forty-nine.'

The woman sighed and shuffled through a pile of pictures in front of her. She selected one and handed it to the general, who passed it to me without saying anything. I stared at it.

I saw a thing with eyes like pale blue pits, many jointed limbs disposed around a blocky body. A cold suspicion began to crush my mind, frigid, petrifying.

I said, 'What has a picture of one of the sky-monsters to do with —'

Suvorov's brown eyes were suddenly full of melting pity, and his voice was gentle as he interrupted me.

'No, Mr Drummond. That is not a sky-monster. That — so far as we can establish — is the present form of your brother Leon Drummond.'

8

I said, 'My — my *brother*?' And had to finish the question in my mind, because I couldn't bear to hear the words spoken aloud.

My brother turned to a many-legged monster? How? In the name of God, how?

For a long while — it seemed an eternity — the sound hung in the still air. No one moved or spoke. I could not even blink my eyes, I was so horribly fascinated by the picture in my hand.

Suddenly Carmen broke the spell. She snatched the photograph from me and looked at it. Her mouth worked. Her eyes widened.

And then she screamed.

It was the most dreadful noise I had ever heard in my life — a raw, throat-tearing cry as uncontrollable as sobbing, but *fierce*. In the low-ceilinged, rock-walled room its echoes battered back at us.

I would have moved to comfort her, put my arm round her or uttered soothing words, but for the moment I was still too dazed. Suvorov, to whom this horror had long ago ceased to be a surprise, reacted at once. He brought the flat of his spade-shaped hand against her cheek with surgical accuracy. The slap, like a switch operating, ended the screaming, and Carmen's eyes closed as she rocked on her heels. The patch of cheek he had hit began to colour angry red against the pallor of the rest of her face.

'Sorry,' Suvorov said curtly. 'But hysteria is the last thing we need right now.'

'If you've quite finished, General . . .' ventured the woman standing at the table.

'Yes, of course. We'll go somewhere out of your way.' He turned to us. 'Come on, let's leave these people in peace. They have rather a lot on their minds.'

Brian, his hand shaking a little, rescued the photograph of what was alleged to be Leon from Carmen's lax grasp the instant before she let it fall, and asked with his eyes whether he might take it with him. The woman standing at the table gave an impatient shrug of permission, and he fell in behind Suvorov as the latter made for the door. I stepped to Carmen's side, put my hand on her arm, and urged her gently to accompany us. She obeyed like a marionette, unsteadily placing one foot in front of the other, not looking where she was going.

Again Suvorov led us down a stone-walled corridor carved from the heart of the mountain, this time bringing us to what was obviously a technical section where armour-glass windows faced on to the actual port. We caught a glimpse of the night outside, the floodlights and the work in progress on the rocket ferries, as he gestured us into a small brightly lit office.

There were just enough chairs for all of us to sit down. He took his place behind a bare desk and slid a box of cigarettes towards us before tilting back his own chair and running his hands through his cropped brown hair.

He said, 'Believe me, you aren't as shocked at this moment as we were a week ago.'

The statement sounded to me like a lie, lost as I was in my white fog of dismay. How could anyone be more shocked than I was — or Carmen, whose trembling I could feel through my fingers, whose teeth I could clearly hear chattering? But my mind was too numb for me to be able to say what I was thinking.

I looked at Brian, envying the fact that he had no brother among the crew. He was leaning forward with his elbows on his knees, staring down at the picture he held in both hands. He was visibly sweating, but he sounded calm enough when he spoke.

Without raising his eyes, he said, 'Are they all like this?'

Carmen tensed fractionally, victim of an access of futile hope. But Suvorov said, 'They differ in details, that's all. Not one of them has escaped the change.'

'Why?' Brian snapped. 'How?'

'What do you think we're trying to find out?' Suvorov countered. He took a cigarette, not from the box he'd offered us but from his pocket: a long Russian one with a built-in pasteboard holder. Having bent the tube at right angles, he lit it and continued out of a cloud of smoke.

'You still understand, I hope, that telling you the facts isn't giving you a licence to publish them? Your argument is probably that the officially imposed silence gives rumours a chance to spread – but what rumours could be worse than a truth of this kind?'

Brian slapped the picture down on the desk with an angry gesture. He said. 'I don't believe in lies, General! White, or any other colour! You're going to have to do better than this before I shut my mouth. You're going to have to tell me a great deal more.'

'If I knew more, I'd tell you,' Suvorov snapped. 'Do you think we're miracle workers? Try me with a question or two, and I'll promise to be honest about our ignorance. Will that suit you?'

Realizing that Suvorov was close to losing his temper, Brian spoke again in a less forceful tone. He said, 'Have you no idea, at least, whether this change is a natural consequence of starflight? For instance, have the interior fittings of the ship changed along with the crew?'

It was an important question and deserved an answer, but that was the moment when I found my own voice, and burst out, 'How can that *thing* be my brother? What grounds have you for saying so?'

Suvorov closed his eyes, the Russian cigarette jutting up from the corner of his mouth. He said, 'They aren't equipped for normal speech at present, and there are psychological problems — what those are exactly I can't say because I'm not an expert. Though who the hell *is* an expert on this?' he added with sudden violence. 'But most of them can write fairly well. He's one of the ones who can.' He pointed at the desk top without looking.

'Excuse me,' Carmen said thinly. 'Why are you talking as though these things are people in different forms? Why are you sure they're not alien creatures that have taken the place of the crew?'

Suvorov said tiredly, 'Did you have a message from your brother, Miss Iglesias? Some messages have been released.'

Carmen nodded.

'Did it strike you as being in character?'

'Yes.'

'So did mine,' I cut in, 'but that proves nothing. The message could have been faked by someone who'd studied up on the psychology of the crewmen before departure.' I sounded doubtful even to myself. Could anyone have selected that of all possible comments — except Leon, whom it fitted so well I could practically hear his voice speaking it, slightly bored, slightly mocking, but patiently accepting the need for long surveillance after their journey into the unknown . . . and contriving to slip a double meaning into it, moreover: a reference not just to the intensive study he was undergoing, but also to the giant faces in the sky!

But before I could pursue my point any further, Suvorov opened his eyes and gave a weary sigh. 'Why are you so ready to assume we're against you, Drummond? We're on your side, damn it. We're just as eager to get to the bottom of the problem as you are. We haven't achieved much so far because, of all the emergencies we prepared for, this wasn't on the list. Suppose you give me five minutes without interruption and I'll tell you all I can.'

The first inkling that something was amiss came when *Starventure* swung within voice communication range of the tugs sent out to gentle her into orbit, and continued to transmit code instead of switching to radio. But in the excitement of the moment no serious notice was taken; it was assumed that an equipment breakdown must accoun for the anomaly.

The tugs brought *Starventure* into orbit, and silence followed.

Alarmed, the expedition commander requested permission to break regulations and send a boarding party across. With the vanishingly small but dangerous risk that there might be alien infection in the starship, no direct contact had been scheduled in that direction; members of the starship's crew were supposed to sterilize their suits and transship to the tugs, remaining sealed from the tugs' atmosphere until after the initial medical examination.

Permission having been granted, volunteers went to investigate, and found the suiting chamber of *Starventure's* main airlock occupied by two apparently monstrous creatures in a state of total catalepsy. The men must have been brave. Though they were unarmed, they declined to turn back. They reported their findings and continued into the ship, finding everything normal except the crew. It was some little while before they came on any more of the latter. When they did, the meeting was perfectly crazy.

Apparently — so Suvorov informed us on the basis of what the psychologists had established — none of the crewmen had had any idea they were physically altered until they were confronted with irrefutable evidence. The pair found in coma in the suiting chamber were examples of this. They had gone to put on spacesuits, intending to jet across to the tugs, and found that they had too many limbs and their bodies were the wrong shape. The shock paralyzed them, and they were found still overcome with fright.

When other members of the crew met the boarding party, they reacted as normal human beings would — provided they had none of their colleagues for reference and comparison. A single crewman would come happily to greet his fellow humans, and be dismayed at their alarm. Two or more together realized by looking at the newcomers and then at each other what had happened to them, and the result was again cataleptic shock.

Naturally, the first explanation that sprang to mind — Suvorov told us with irony — was the one which Carmen had just voiced: that the crew had somehow been replaced during the trip with alien beings. In a sense, of course, this was so. The human bodies of the crew had been transformed, or exchanged, or . . . *something*.

But it rapidly became clear that the personalities of the crew were still present, reflected in their strange new shapes. Not all of them could talk; those who could spoke in the wrong auditory range. But they could all communicate with each other and retained the ability to write. It was as though some areas of common human experience had been blanked off for them, whereas other areas which might not be human at all had been opened up for them.

'This is why the psychologists are having such difficulty,' Suvorov said. 'For instance, although the bodies in which the crew's minds now seem to be — ah — housed are much more different one from another than human bodies, having various types and numbers of limbs, various distribution of bodily organs, and so on, they all share the ability to sense radiant energy far down into the ultraviolet. We're still testing them; some of them may be able to "see" X-rays. And another thing: some of them appreciate the passage of time differently from us. We had to send up a computer to handle the questioning of the one who's been identified as Chandra Dan; at first we thought he was one of the ones who can't talk, but then it turned out he was compressing whole sentences into tiny fractions of a second. Don't ask me for details — I'm just relaying to you what little I've managed to absorb.'

'What became of the ones who went into catalepsy?' Brian demanded.

'Oh, the initial shock wore off remarkably quickly. In a day or so at most they became able to adjust, and now they're moving round among the people who've been sent up to study them, and proving perfectly compliant.'

'Are these new bodies of theirs oxygen-breathing?'

'Yes, they're quite happy in Earth-normal air. Also they utilize ordinary food, though they seem to need a high proportion of extra trace elements, particularly cobalt and manganese.'

Brian frowned and gave a nod. 'David here was telling me that there have been more takeoffs than landings from the port recently. What have you been doing — sending up teams of investigators?'

'Yes, of course, and a great deal of equipment too. And we've had to leave three or four of our ferries in orbit, locked on to *Starventure*, to accommodate everything.'

'When were they . . .?' began Carmen, ran out of breath on a whisper of terror, and tried again. 'When were they *changed*?'

'During the return trip. Probably, just before their re-emergence into normal space. We have the pictures they took in the Centaurus system, and some of those show members of the crew normally suited up, which would of course have been impossible if the change had taken place there. And we have a few records from the voyage home, mainly of instrument readings, which include a glimpse of normal hands or fingers.'

'Have they no recollection at all of the — the process?' Brian asked.

'None at all.'

Brian gazed down at the picture of what was alleged to be my brother. I still hadn't come to grips with that idea. He said, 'David thought this was a picture of a sky-monster when you first showed it to him. What's the connection between these bodies and the shapes we've been seeing in the sky? The resemblance is remarkable, isn't it?'

Silently I damned him for being so cool when I was on the edge of a precipice of insane terror.

Suvorov shook his head, looking unutterably fatigued. He said, 'How can we know? We have only one working hypothesis, and I don't understand it, but for what it's worth . . . Well, it's been suggested that there are creatures in hyperspace, intelligent, possessed of vast knowledge and power, to whom a body has no individuality but is simply regarded as a vehicle for the mind. By some means we can't fathom, we attracted their attention when we launched *Starventure* into their universe. On the outward trip they were taken by surprise, so that it wasn't until the return trip that they were able to abstract the crew's bodies in order to examine them, replacing them with what they thought would be satisfactory substitutes. Now they've tracked the ship to Earth itself, and they're looking us over. Owing to the different physical qualities of the universe they inhabit, we see them projected on the sky.'

Brian blinked, and appealed to me for comment. 'David, how does that strike you? I can see it making a sort of twisted sense, but it scares me.'

'The word I agree with is "twisted",' I said, wiping my face with the back of my hand. 'It'd call for a whole new cosmology to accommodate the idea. And right now I can't think straight enough to give an option.'

Brian turned to Suvorov again. He said, 'I hate to have to admit this, but — well, maybe it is better not to publish the facts until we know a great deal more. But you can't make do with mere denials. You're going to have to release some kind of story to the press, preferably something with a lot of half-truths in it, amplified convincingly enough to stifle all these rumours that are going around.'

I took a deep breath. I'd never in my life expected to want to connive at hiding important truths from the world, but I was compelled to agree with Brian. Something as shattering as what we'd just been told was too great a shock to release all at once; the ground would have to be prepared.

I said, 'Yes, Brian, I'm afraid you're right. And I — I guess I could help you write the proper kind of lies. In fact I'll agree to do so on one condition.'

Suvorov looked at me expressionlessly.

'I'd like to — to meet my brother.'

The words hung in the air like smoke for a long moment. But finally the general gave a nod.

'I think I can arrange that,' he said. 'It will be worth it to have the authority of a Kalinga Prize winner behind this misleading news story. Does Miss Iglesias also want the chance to see her brother?'

We all glanced at Carmen. After a pause she shook back her sleek dark hair and set her chin mutinously.

'See my brother?' she echoed. 'Of course not. No matter what you say, I know it isn't my brother who's up there in the ship. I've seen him myself in Quito — not as a monster, but as himself, alive and well.'

Suvorov leapt to his feet as though stuck with a goad. 'For God's sake!' he exclaimed. 'Why didn't you tell us that before?'

9

I had been on the point of apologizing for the foolishness of
Carmen's remark. Suvorov's reaction startled me, and a
moment later I was very glad I hadn't spoken.

Before, it had of course seemed ridiculous on the face of
it to think that I might *really* have seen Leon — Leon's body
— in Quito, or that Carmen and her nephew might have
seen Hermanos. Indeed, in spite of her requests that I
inquire among the other relatives of the crew for people
who had had similar visions, I'd only made a show of
complying, thinking that there were many other lines of
investigation which demanded my attention. I hadn't even
mentioned the point, that I could recall, to Brian, Kaye or
Don, who were old colleagues of mine and could certainly
have found time to check with the many members of crewmen's families who were now converging on Quito.

'Explain clearly, please, Miss Iglesias,' Suvorov ordered.
'When and under what circumstances did you see what you
took for your brother?'

Still pale with shock, still having to interlace her fingers
to stop them trembling, but speaking in a calm enough
tone, Carmen said, 'Not only I, but a nephew of mine also,
a boy six years old.'

'All the more interesting. Go on.'

She recited her story, and finished by turning to me.

'The same thing happened to you, didn't it, David?'

Sheepishly I admitted that was so.

'Why didn't you report this earlier?' Suvorov snapped.

'Well . . . Henri Chambord knew,' I muttered, feeling
peculiarly guilty, as though I'd withheld valuable evidence
at a trial where Leon's life was in danger.

Suvorov jabbed at a button on his desk and leaned back
in his chair. He said, 'I have no idea whether this is important, but certainly to me it is new. Any new fact may be
valuable.'

Carmen glanced at me, her head tilted a little, one eyebrow lifted. I guessed what she was thinking. She had said

almost exactly the same thing to me when asking me to make those inquiries among the families of the crew.

'By the way,' Suvorov added, 'everything you said during our talk has been recorded. We've been on twenty-four-hour recording since the ship returned to normal space. On the record, I want to warn you formally that everything I've told you which has not been released to the press is UN-classified and divulgence of it will result in withdrawal of all your UN privileges. Signify you understand this warning.'

We muttered that we did. It was chastening to move over from the privileged reporter's seat to the ordinary layman's rôle, but I could all too easily visualize the terror which might follow the wrongly timed release of this appalling news, and neither my heart nor Brian's was in objecting.

The desk phone sounded. Suvorov flipped the switch and said, 'Is Dr Lenister there?'

The sound was directionalized and we couldn't hear the answer, but it must have been affirmative, for he continued, 'Ask him to step into my office for a few minutes, will you? I have something new for him, I think.'

Brian asked me a question with his eyes.

'Herb Lenister,' I said. 'Cornell and Sorbonne. Cybernetic psychologist. Just one of about a hundred scientists I've been trying to talk to this past week.'

If I'd known what they knew, I concluded silently to myself, *I'd have decided not to bother them.*

Lenister turned up almost at once: a dapper man, extremely well dressed, with half-rimmed glasses and a gold tooth. He looked worn out, though, which wasn't surprising. He sat on the corner of Suvorov's desk and nodded acknowledgment of the introductions.

'All right, what's the urgent news?' he said.

'Miss Iglesias here — sister of Hermanos Iglesias aboard *Starventure* — reports seeing her brother in Quito the day of the re-emergence.'

Lenister sighed. 'Yes, I know,' he said. 'So did her nephew a day later, and Drummond reported something similar to the press officer, Chambord.'

'You knew?' Brian demanded. 'How did you hear?'

Lenister took off his glasses and wiped them carefully. 'Oh, stories like that get around a town which is bubbling the way Quito is at the moment. And we've been collecting every scrap of data we can find, regardless of whether it's fact or rumour.'

'But what have you done to follow up the stories?' Brian persisted.

'Follow them up? Jesus Christ almighty, Mr Watchett, when do you think we might have found the *time*?' Lenister rammed his glasses back into place. 'We have a whole department investigating strange coincidences, alleged precognitive dreams, silly-season newspaper stories, things of that kind, on the slim chance that we may dig up some kind of link between them all. But think what we've also got to cope with that's a deal more solid! Solar disturbances! Auroral phenomena! Magnetic anomalies! Cosmic ray showers! The re-entry of *Starventure* played merry hell with the continuum across three-quarters of the solar system. With respect, Miss Iglesias, we have other things on our minds than locating a double for your brother.'

'But nothing more important,' Brian said.

Poised to rise from Suvorov's desk and leave, Lenister blinked at him in surprise. 'I don't think I understand,' he said after a moment.

I'd seen the look on Brian's face before. He was playing a hunch, reading into what Lenister had said something that a thousand other people would have failed to notice.

'I hadn't heard about Miss Iglesias's brother, or Leon Drummond. But I had heard about people who thought they'd seen other members of the crew in Quito — I've had similar stories from four or five sources since my arrival. I checked up and found that none of the sources was personally acquainted with the crewmen they claimed to have seen, so I put it down to overactive imagination. Now I'm not so sure any longer.'

Carmen said breathlessly, 'The day the ship came back, David and I were the only people in Quito — apart from the rest of my family — related to a member of the crew.'

'But granting that,' Lenister said, 'I still don't know why Mr Watchett thinks it's terribly important.'

'Nor do I,' I said, butting in before Brian could respond. 'Look, Brian! Are you implying that the — the *real* bodies of the crew could have been seen here, with alien minds in control?'

Annoyed, as though he'd expected me to support him

without question, Brian said, 'Well, there are a hell of a lot of bodies missing, aren't there?'

'So how were they put down on Earth? In a ship? Tossed down through the atmosphere like meteorites?'

'Damn it!' He sat up furiously straight. 'You're the scientific brain between us two — why not through hyperspace, though?'

My mouth opened and no words came out. Why not, indeed? We were still only trespassing on the fringe of that mysterious domain.

'Gentlemen,' Lenister said, 'I sympathize, believe me. You've only just been exposed to the problem. We've had it for a full week now, and we're still learning to discard traditional preconceptions. Mr Watchett may be perfectly right, and the missing bodies of the crew may be here on Earth — may even have been landed via hyperspace, for all I know. But, for pity's sake, we've *got* the crew in their new shapes, up there at *Starventure*, and we still have to find out a million and one things about them! Are we to divert our efforts from that to chase after these crew members' doubles, vouched for only by one man, or one woman, or a six-year-old boy?'

'But I think it's worth investigating, as Mr Watchett argued,' put in Suvorov. 'For all we know, doctor, one of those monsters might have reached down from the sky and set the crew's bodies on their feet like a kid playing with toy soldiers.'

Once more Lenister wiped his glasses, this time very slowly and tiredly.

'Yes, yes of course,' he muttered. 'But I haven't anyone to spare to look into such matters more than we're doing already.'

'I'll take care of it,' Brian said. 'If we put out this cover story we've been talking about, there won't be any honest news to keep me busy for a while.'

'Cover story?' Lenister said questioningly, and I summed up what Brian and I had agreed to do.

'Excellent idea,' he approved. 'Though I haven't the vaguest idea what you're going to say. But the sooner you do it, the better. So I'll get back to work. Forgive me if I've been sharp with you, but I'm sure you appreciate the strain we're all under.'

We said we did, and he went out.

62

Suvorov cleared his throat as the door closed. He said, 'A point has occurred to me, Mr Drummond. You set a price on your co-operation, a chance to visit your brother. I can set that up for tomorrow or the next day. But there must be an impregnable excuse for your absence. It must not be allowed to leak out that you've been allowed to visit *Starventure* when none of the other relatives of crewmen has even been permitted to enter the spaceport.'

'I can fix that,' I said. 'I can rely on Brian to spread some misleading excuses, can't I?' — I glanced his way — 'and there are some people in the Prensam office here who'll say anything I ask and not want to know why.'

I snapped my fingers and added, 'I can always put it about that I've been sent by Hank Sandler for first-hand coverage of the monster sightings in Chile.'

'Don't trouble me with the details,' Suvorov said. 'Just make sure the story's watertight.' He checked his watch. 'I'd better get you back to Quito now. I'm due on duty in less than ten minutes, so I'll have to send you home with a staff driver. Will you be going to see Chambord?'

Brian nodded. 'We can't put together our cover story without his help. He's going to have to play Joseph to it, poor devil — which he certainly isn't going to enjoy.'

He made to rise. Suvorov held out his hand, but not to shake with him.

'That photograph, please, Mr Watchett! It's an unbreakable rule that such a thing must not be allowed to leave the port.'

Brian parted with the shiny sheet reluctantly. He said, 'You know, the more I look at that picture, the more I'm convinced that none of what you've told me can be true.'

'I'm sure that will be a great help in preparing your cover story,' Suvorov commented ironically. 'By the way, one last point: you must of course let our experts know what you intend to say. You don't know the entire story even now, so there's a risk of your inventing something which is dangerously close to the truth. So send in your draft before you show it to Chambord, even, and never mind what time of day or night you have it ready. We shall have plenty of competent authorities to approve it. We have more top scientific talent within three miles of this spot, getting less sleep for a longer time, than ever in human history.'

'And if you don't like what we suggest?' I had to say that,

but a moment later, I regretted it. For when Suvorov turned his face to me, it was the face of a haunted man.

'We shall have to like it, shan't we?' he said quietly. 'Really, we have no choice. It's that, or worldwide hysteria. Goodbye for the present, then. I shall expect to hear from you in a few hours' time.'

I helped Carmen, who was death-pale still, to her feet. Then, like pallbearers under the weight of a giant's coffin, we stumbled out into the night.

10

Our new driver made the return trip at a more reasonable speed than Suvorov when he was bringing us, but after what we had learned we were in no mood to be grateful for that. It might almost have been better to be pitched to our deaths uncaring than to confront this strange and terrible new universe.

I didn't say or do anything for at least a couple of miles, but simply watched the rocky wall beside the road loom up, sidestep, vanish as the car's lights played over it. At last I stirred and made to put my arm comfortingly around Carmen's shoulders. It was like touching a wax dummy. When I looked at her, at first I could not see her face; then, as the road curved, the car's lights were thrown back and shed a brief illumination over us. Her eyes were wide, fixed straight ahead, and her lips were moving in soundless speech.

I said, 'Carmen!'

She ignored me for a long moment. I guessed she must be reciting a prayer and taking the time to finish it. That was a new thing to me; I had never had any idea she was religious.

'Leave me alone,' she said in a voice as dead as the moon.

I tried to object. She turned her head slowly – I could see as once again the headlights were reflected by rocks at the roadside – and bared her teeth in a near-snarl.

'David, you don't own me,' she said. 'Leave me alone.'

Once more I had the sensation of seeing her for the first

time. Compliantly I withdrew my arm, feeling a sudden stab of misery as sharp as at the news of an old friend's death. It seemed for the instant impossible that I should ever meet my Carmen again: laughing, affectionate, excited by me and by the world.

But Brian, leaning back in the seat beside the driver, was saying something, and I had to tear my attention free and direct it to him. I said, 'I'm sorry, I didn't catch that.'

'I was asking if you have any definite ideas about the line we should take with Chambord. It's going to be hard to enlist his co-operation.'

I put up my hand to rub my forehead.

'Ah . . . no,' I said at length. 'Sorry. I'm still pretty shaken up by what's happened to Leon. I'll have to rely on you for ideas until I recover.'

'It seems to me there's only one possibility. Here, have a cigarette.' He half turned to reach the pack towards me, then twisted further to offer it to Carmen. I pushed his arm back.

'She wants to be left alone,' I muttered emptily. 'Go on.'

He fumbled on the dashboard for the car's lighter. 'Well, it's ridiculous' — he puffed smoke — 'to try and pretend that nothing's gone wrong. We have to pick on the least damaging of the convincing reasons for the long delay in the crew's return to Earth. About the only thing I can think of right now is this quarantine I understand that they were supposed to undergo. What's the chance of their being infected with some alien organism, so that they can't land until the experts find a cure?'

'A million to one against is the lowest odds I've been quoted,' I said with a sigh. 'Anyway, the quarantine gimmick stinks. It'll be taken for granted that the crew are all at death's door. Their families will scream blue murder, and what's worse every biologist on Earth will prick up his ears and start howling for data on this marvellous alien bacterium. Something from another planet capable of preying on terrestrial protoplasm would be the biggest news of the century in biology, biochemistry, paleobiology . . . No, we couldn't sustain a lie like that.'

Brain slapped his open palm on his knee. 'Damned fools!' he exploded. 'Sometimes I think it's true what they used to say about scientists living in an ivory tower! Wouldn't you have thought that the moment the boarding party found what had happened to the starship's crew they'd have realized a fiction like this would become necessary? If they'd only taken some competent PR man like Henri into their confidence right away, they'd have saved us having to build on seven days' worth of half-truths and falsehoods!'

I nodded agreement.

'Well, let's see,' Brian went on, scowling worse than ever. 'What about psychological breakdown? They couldn't endure the stresses of the unfamiliar environment of hyperspace.'

'Oh, Brian, for heaven's sake!' I muttered. 'You must be even more worn out than I am. Can't you see what's wrong with that? Damn it, people still have this instinctive revulsion against insanity; you couldn't put it about that the crew had been unbalanced by their experience without undermining public support for any kind of spaceflight.'

'Don't you think that's going to happen anyway?' Brian said softly.

I tried not to admit even to myself that his prediction was likely to be right. It wasn't that I myself had much personal involvement with spaceflight — I'd never been further than orbit — but Leon did, and maybe to a greater extent than I'd formerly recognized, Leon represented my proxy, making the progress in science which I'd hoped to make myself but which circumstances compelled me only to report.

In any case, *Starventure* had been seen as an achievement of the 'because it's there' type, possibly the first in history in which the whole population of the world had a vicarious share. No matter how ingenious a lie we concocted, the disappointment at our failure was going to be appalling.

I said, 'I don't think the idea would work for another reason, you know. People would promptly start asking why, if hyperspace is so intolerable, the crew managed to survive the outward trip, when the strain would have been much worse because they were bound for an unknown destination. On the way home, there would have been journey's end to look forward to.'

'Blast it, you're right,' Brian conceded. By this time his eyebrows were nearly meeting above his nose. 'Well, it's your turn now since you've shot down my first suggestions.'

Suppose you stop moping and start thinking — or have you got out of the habit since you set up in business on your own?'

By the time we re-entered the city, we had the skeleton of our story, which could be developed according to circumstances in three ways: it could prepare the world for the truth, it could become a permanent lie with downbeat implications designed to depress public interest in future starflights and discourage questions about the first one, or on the billion-to-one level it could be dropped and forgotten in a day following a resolution of the problem through some new discovery.

I was so engrossed in fleshing out this skeleton, feeling a kind of perverse pleasure in my own unexpected ingenuity, that I almost forgot about Carmen. When I suddenly realized how long it was since I'd even glanced at her, we had turned off the main road towards Chambord's home, where Suvorov had of course instructed our driver to take us first.

I tapped him on the shoulder and told him in Spanish to pull up. Turning to Carmen, I asked if I should find her a cab to take her home.

She nodded without speaking. The driver suggested backing up to the highway again, because there were more likely to be cabs there than here, but Carmen simply opened her door and climbed out.

I jumped out after her and tried to catch her by the arm, but she avoided me. I said, 'Carmen! Why are you treating me as though it's all my fault?'

'You think I'm lying to you,' she said stonily. 'I did see my brother, as clearly as you saw yours. Not a vision, not a monster, but my Hermanos alive and well.'

The weight of her words crushed my mind. What the devil was I to do? I hesitated, wondering whether to send Brian to see Chambord by himself and leave me to take Carmen home and comfort her; she was clearly in a state of extreme shock.

But, all of a sudden, she conjured up a smile and laid a hand on my arm. 'Dear David!' she said. 'Go and do what you have to do, and don't worry about me. I shall be all right. Look, there's a cab right now!'

She had spotted, with eyesight that had sometimes surprised me before, the faint distant glow of a lighted sign on a car roof. Breaking loose from me, she ran towards the highway shouting and waving. The driver spotted her and slowed down.

Hurrying after her, unable to catch her up, I called out. 'Carmen! Don't go home by yourself and brood! Go and spend the night with your family!'

I couldn't be sure whether she heard me, but she waved and slipped into the back seat of the cab, which took off with a roar and shortly was lost to sight.

Turning back to rejoin Brian, I wondered whether my idea had been such a good one after all. The vision of Carmen fighting her personal devils alone in her apartment through the darkest hours of night had prompted me to suggest it. But it was, come to think of it, from her family that she had this streak of — what to call it — mysticism, credulity, superstition . . .

'Think she'll be okay?' Brian asked as I re-entered our car. 'She seemed terribly shaken up.'

'Carmen's just about the most resilient person I know,' I assured him. Which was true, in normal circumstances — she possessed fierce independence and inexhaustible determination. But what was there that was normal about this situation?

We reached Chambord's home in another few minutes — a new smart bungalow set back from the road in a garden riotous with gaudy flowers. A light was on in one of the front windows, and as we shut the car doors behind us a dark figure appeared in silhouette on the step of the porch.

'David?' Chambord's voice inquired. 'Ah, I heard from General Suvorov that you were coming to see me — and Mr Watchett, I believe. So I presume you have got results from your visit to the base. Please come in, but go quietly because my wife is sleeping at the back of the house.'

He led us into the hallway. There we could see how puffy his eyes were, how haggard his expression, infinitely worse than when we'd spoken with him only a few hours earlier. The sight of his over-tiredness made me check my watch for the first time in hours. I was dismayed to see that it was already well after one A.M.

In the room where we had seen the light on, he gave us chairs and brought us cups of café-cognac. It was exactly what I needed. I felt my head clear and my spirits revive.

'*Eh bien!*' he said, taking another chair facing ours. 'All I know so far is what the general told me: that to forestall further rumours it's been decided to make a further release about the starship, and that you two and I must prepare a draft by eight o'clock this morning. Well, I am ready to listen. Of course, I am certain that what I shall hear isn't going to be palatable.'

He folded his hands on his lap and looked at us expectantly.

Well, now for the first test of our big lie. I cleared my throat; Brian and I had agreed that since I was a science writer I stood the better chance of putting our story over.

'Yes. Well . . . Well, it looks as though our decision to force a showdown coincided with their decision to come clean. It's clear to everyone by now that something has gone wrong, and when we marched in and threatened to raise hell they swung clear around and asked for our co-operation. They've been completely at a loss, apparently, because of some of the effects that the crew have suffered which nobody anticipated, and they simply haven't had time to think about trying to explain things to the public.'

'What sort of effects?' prompted Chambord.

'Partly physical and partly psychological. Remember these are the first men who've spent any length of time in hyperspace, and conditions there are completely different from our normal universe. The psychological effects sound as though they're going to be the easiest to cope with, because the human mind has a limited range of responses to stress. The main trouble is acute agoraphobia. For many of the crew the voyage was unbroken; only a small landing-party set down on the Centauran worlds, and the rest had to stay cooped up for two solid years inside the ship. They simply can't face being brought down to Earth, to large open spaces and sky above their heads. But of course now they're being treated by experts, and that wouldn't present much of a problem if it weren't for the physical effects complicating matters.'

I had to pause and lick my lips.

'You see, just as the pioneer astronauts suffered unforeseen consequences of free fall, such as bone softening due to the piezoelectric effect of gravity on the accumulation of calcium in the skeleton, so there have been metabolic disorders discovered in hyperspace. The tissues of the crew's bodies have been affected; their injuries haven't healed normally, their digestion has been affected, and there are all kinds of other side effects which make it impossible for them to be brought straight back to Earth without grave risk of permanent incapacitation.'

There was a long silence. Finally Chambord gave a nod.

'Very well,' he said. 'If that's the story, I must take it as it stands. But I warn you, I don't believe a word.'

Brian and I exchanged looks of dismay.

'I'll tell you why,' Chambord pursued. 'First of all, David, I am an old hand at detecting a falsehood. I know your work especially well. I can say that in speech you do not use such a word as — oh — "incapacitation". You may write it, because it is precise, but you do not say it. And second, I have been in the UN press service most of my working life. I have seen international crises of all sizes from ruffled diplomatic tempers to incipient nuclear wars, and not one of them has created such a panic. No innocent metabolic disorder could account for what I have seen this past week. Am I perhaps entitled to the truth, even if I have to stand godfather to a lie?'

He shot questioning glances at each of us in turn. 'Well? Are we to be invaded from the stars tomorrow? Did the starship find heaven and learn that mankind is excluded? What then?'

Neither Brian nor I moved a muscle.

'As you prefer,' he sighed. 'Now we must set to work on this story you tell me, and conspire to deceive the public. There are few people who could persuade me to this, you know, David. But if you come to me, even me, and retail me this nonsense, then what has really happened must be very terrible indeed. I am perhaps happier not knowing.'

11

By its third draft that release was a masterpiece. It was thick and ponderous, yet hollow; it was like an elephant made out of fog. It said all kinds of depressing things in a tone of horrible optimism. According to mood, one might read into it, either a permanent epitaph for star-travel, or a paean of praise for the brave members of the crew who had opened the doors of the universe, or a sober and neutral record of fact.

At about five-thirty, red-eyed and shaking with the effort of concentrating on every single word, we got it licked and read it to Suvorov over the phone, using Chambord's scrambler line to the spaceport through which he could take pre-deadline confidential data.

Suvorov recorded it, promised to call together all available heads of department to approve it and left us to await their verdict with all the nervousness of expectant fathers. It came at six-ten: not merely approved, but warmly welcomed because it left so many options open.

Chambord picked up the only draft in existence of our superlative lie and folded it into his pocket, looking gloomy.

'So I will take this down to the press office and have it 'faxed', he said. 'And at eight o'clock it will be released. After which . . .'

'What?' I said, dropping into an armchair because my legs would suddenly not bear my weight.

'After that I think I shall resign!' Chambord snapped and strode out.

'Come to think of it,' Brian said, crossing the room to the phone, 'we ought to call off any hounds Hank still has on the scent.' I nodded. I'd been meaning to suggest it myself, only somehow I hadn't found the energy.

Eight A.M. was just about the right time for the release, I figured. Reaction was likely to be strongest in this hemisphere. The morning papers would have gone out and been read; the noons and evenings would carry it, of course, but the facts would now trickle into the public awareness; hints would have prepared the majority of people before they got the story in full either on leaving work or from seeing a TV bulletin on their arrival home. In Western Europe and Eastern Russia, where reaction was likely to be the strongest, it would hit in the early afternoon, and would again be tempered by leaking through in instalments before TV and the next day's papers filled in the gaps. The reaction in China and Japan was all that worried me, but over that side of Earth there was, after all, a long tradition of respect for the authority of the expert, which I'd just so flagrantly abused.

I closed my eyes, but despite my exhaustion I had no urge to sleep. Across the room I could hear Brian asking our New York office (amazing how rapidly I'd fallen back into the habit of thinking of it as 'our') for Sandler or whoever was on duty. The voice which answered wasn't Sandler's, but I didn't look to see if I recognized the face on the screen.

'Release at eight A.M. your time?' I heard. 'But – hell, our morning editions will be printed and wrapped by then!'

'Tell Hank this is what we got for being pushy,' Brian said in a convincingly dispirited tone. 'He gave me this ultimatum last night, and we acted on it. So we get the release at eight A.M. and a bond of secrecy until then.'

'I've half a mind to rout out Hank and have him draft the piece he planned to do tomorrow! Then we could get the demand for the release on the beams ahead of the actual text. Be good prestige-wise, wouldn't it?'

'Good for nothing else, though. They'd jump to the conclusion I tipped you off, and Solar's press facilities down here would be up the creek. Henri Chambord's in charge. You may have heard of him.'

'Are you joking? Yes, you're right, I'm afraid. I wouldn't put it past Chambord to blacklist even Solar. But can't you at least make sure Kaye gets the text immediately? Then maybe tomorrow's mornings will carry our own version instead of the plain official handout.'

'I guess we could do that,' Brian agreed, wiping his face with one hand and reaching to cut the circuit with the other.

A thought struck me, which would have occurred to me much earlier if I hadn't been two years out of touch. I said, 'Brian, this piece the guy was just talking about – the demand for full details about the ship, yes?'

'Yes. What about it?'

'Whose name was Hank planning to hang on it? His own? It would have needed a name – a plain agency credit wouldn't have got it any space.'

'Since when has a Solar bureau chief used his own name on a story?' Brian countered wryly. 'And what would it mean to the public if he did? No, the question's academic, but in fact he was going to use your name as a peg. I was supposed to talk you into giving permission. It would have gone out as a straight release, not a Solar feature, licensed for unlimited rewriting, in the hope of catching the public mood and sparking off a worldwide reaction.'

'Hank's a clever bastard,' I said. The trick might have worked, too, and it hadn't even occurred to me. I forced myself out of my chair and stretched to the tips of my toes.

'Well, that's that,' I said around a yawn.

'No, it's not,' Brian contradicted, swivelling round on the stool by the phone. 'I took on a job, remember? I propose to start right now. I want the fullest details you can remember concerning your encounter with your brother the day of *Starventure's* return.'

Slowly I sank back into the chair I'd just left. I said, 'I wish to God you'd mentioned these other stories you'd heard. I might have taken my own experience a bit more seriously.'

'As of now, you take it seriously,' Brian said. He took out his recorder, checked that there was a clean crystal in it, and set it going.

'And when you've finished telling me about seeing Leon,' he concluded, 'you can tell me what you know about your friend Carmen and her nephew. I'm determined to get to the bottom of this.'

It was almost eight when I got back to my hotel. I bought all the available papers and took them up to my room. While I was filling a tub to soak away my exhaustion, I leafed through them. The two big stories of the day were connected, I knew that for certain now. I wondered how many people were making the connection by guesswork.

Some amateur radio-astronomers, doing daytime work on meteor reflections, had found unaccountable short-range signals bouncing back from just the other side of the blue sky, as though there were something solid there, such as a sky-monster. One of the papers had contrived to reach Professor Acosta, which surprised me, and secured from him a grudging admission that other similar phenomena had previously been observed.

And in Jakarta the parents of one of *Starventure's* engineers had been provoked into making accusations of deception against the officials at the starship base. There was a four-column picture in most of the papers showing a

73

very handsome middle-aged woman weeping over a bunch of flowers.

Scowling, I turned off the tub and went to the phone. I called Carmen's family's number, which I still had from my previous visits to Quito. I got her mother on the line. She spoke no English, and what with my lack of fluency in Spanish and her Indian accent and vocabulary it took a hell of a long time to make myself understood, but eventually I discovered that Carmen had indeed spent the night there, and also that she had gone out a quarter of an hour earlier, presumably intending to go to work. I thanked Sra Iglesias and tried Carmen's office number, but got no reply. It was barely eight, and the staff, I figured, wouldn't be in yet. I decided to take my bath and try again at half past.

Wondering who it was who had managed to break down Acosta's reticence, I checked that story again, and was pleased to see that one of Manuel Segura's staffers had the byline. That meant, naturally, Solar had the North American rights if they wanted them. It was ridiculous how quickly the habits due to two years of freelancing had faded; I was once again a loyal Solar Press employee — for the time being.

I wasn't sure I liked being an employee of any kind.

Throwing aside the papers, I stared through the steamy air at nothing in particular. Thinking of Manuel had reminded me that I was supposed to plant a cover story for myself, as well as the grand one, to disguise my absence in space. From my mental note to call him and request his help, my mind had suddenly leaped to the impending reality of that trip.

Now I was beginning to sense a little of what Carmen must have endured last night. I whispered under my breath, trying to make facts come real by dressing them in words.

'Listen! Today, or more likely tomorrow, they're going to take you down to the spaceport and load you on an orbital ferry and fly you out to *Starventure*. There they are going to show you a — a creature, a half-shapeless thing with metallic eyes and too many limbs, which they will say is Leon. How can it *possibly* be Leon?'

I'd been in space before, so the flight itself didn't frighten me. But the thought of what was promised to me out there brought back visions from the past. By the time I was old enough to take notice, the Mars flight was a routine matter and there were permanent colonists on the Moon. I was vaguely aware, though, that in the early days of spaceflight some people had seriously feared the consequences — whether for the comparatively rational reason that Mars might be inhabited by dangerous monsters, or because they regarded the heavens as God's private domain and spacemen as impious trespassers.

Well, so far God had kept quiet. But here were the monsters with a vengeance.

The phone went. I started, making the water in the tub slosh back and forth with little waves that broke against my chest. I'd forgotten to switch my incoming calls through to the sound-only circuit serving the bathroom. For a minute I was inclined to let it ring; then I realized it might be Carmen calling and climbed out of the bath.

Swathed in towels, leaving wet footprints on the carpet, I went to answer. It wasn't Carmen. A uniformed man showed in the screen.

'Mr Drummond?'

'Yes — what is it?'

'General Suvorov for you. Hold the line.'

The screen blanked; then the image re-formed, catching Suvorov passing his fingers tiredly through his hair.

'Good morning, Mr Drummond,' he said. 'We owe you our congratulations — you and Mr Watchett. Your cover story is exactly what the situation called for.'

'How long it will stand up is anybody's guess.' I shrugged. 'Henri Chambord saw through it right away.'

'At least it has gained us a breathing space. So I will fulfill my part of our bargain, not only because I am a man of my word but also because when I put the idea to our psychologists they said it would be very helpful to study the reaction not only of yourself to your brother in his — ah — new shape, but also of your brother himself.'

I said nothing. The water drying on my skin was chilling me despite the warmth of the air.

'We have an orbital shot scheduled for 1650 hours this afternoon. Please report to the spaceport at noon for a medical examination and to be kitted out. Have you flown space before?'

I must have gaped. Luckily the picture-melt didn't catch me, so Suvorov didn't see my surprise. But either he had been pulling strings very hard, or the psychologists up at the ship were ready to grasp at any straw.

Swallowing, I contrived to answer. 'Yes, a couple of times. No further than orbit, though.'

'That's where you'll be going this time. I've made no arrangements for Miss Iglesias, by the way. I judged by her attitude last night that she might be unco-operative.'

'I don't think she would want to go,' I agreed.

The picture-melt caught me with a dispirited expression; I was very unhappy about Carmen right now. Suvorov, frozen in a frown, commented.

'Did you get any sleep last night?' he demanded.

'No.'

'Then take an hour's forced-sleep before you come out to the port. Otherwise the doctors will veto your flight. And have you arranged this excuse for your absence which I asked for?'

'I was intending to, directly I'd had my bath. But I just realized: I didn't ask how long I'm likely to be away.'

'Twenty-four hours, not longer.'

'All right. Shall I make my own way to the port, or will you send a car for me?'

'I'll have a car waiting for you at eleven-thirty.'

When he had broken the connection, it didn't seem worth getting back in the tub. I dried and put on clean clothes and returned to the phone. First I ordered breakfast and asked someone to go to the chemist's and get me some forced-sleep capsules, and then I called Manuel Segura.

After congratulating him on getting one of his men into Acosta's office, I mentioned casually that since, after the morning news release, it didn't look as though there would be many further developments here for a while, I was considering dropping down to Chile to check up on the first of the epidemic of sky-monsters. That started him off on a recital of the latest monsters to be reported, and without my saying anything more I was sure by the time he was through that he'd remember me promising to disappear to Chile for at least a day and possibly longer. I could rely on Brian to reinforce the impression.

So that was taken care of. And by now, surely, Carmen must have arrived at work.

I called the firm again, and this time a pretty receptionist answered me. No, Señorita Iglesias had not come in this

76

morning. No, she had not called to say she was unwell. She had simply not put in an appearance. They had called her home to inquire, but her mother had been very surprised to learn she wasn't at work. Was there any message?

Dismayed, I mumbled something and rang off.

12

What had that crazy girl taken it into her head to do now?

I'd always pictured Carmen as being one of the most levelheaded and self-possessed people I knew. She had seemed to me to look on life from a refreshingly cynical viewpoint — not unpleasantly cynical, but wry, detached, tolerant of human failings.

Now all of a sudden I found myself wondering whether part of my opinion had been due to a kind of sociological trick of the light. Latin America was, after all, still a very conservative area of the world; possibly part of my image of Carmen was due to her being somewhat more emancipated than the average . . .?

I couldn't be sure. What I could be certain of, however was that what had happened to her brother had stripped away a mask and laid bare beneath something archetypally older. She had talked of having second sight because she was the seventh child of a seventh child, but I'd never regarded that as being meant to be taken seriously. I'd dismissed it as a pose adopted *pour épater les scientistes* — like me — and if circumstances had been different I'd have gone on thinking so.

Now, having had my own nice tidy world-picture blown to smithereens, I was even beginning to wonder how much of a joke it had been when she talked of her ancestry being one-quarter jaguar.

I spent a few terrifying minutes thinking about the changes that were going to take place in the world I'd known. All my life I'd believed in the ideal of progress — that we were ridding ourselves of an ancient burden, replacing superstition and dogma with reason and fact. I remembered the ringing phrases I'd used to describe *Starventure's* return, about 'man throwing down his challenge to the stars', and I shivered.

It looked as though the stars had failed to recognize our challenge, and the outcome would be the collapse of all our pride.

I'd shared that pride. Somewhere in the back of my mind, and I imagined in the minds of most people of this twenty-first century, there had been a dream of Man encompassing the universe by the power of his intelligence. That was the vision which had inspired *Starventure*.

Could we have been deluding ourselves? Had we truly been misled into thinking that because we seemed to understand our own little corner of the cosmos we were on the way to understanding the whole of it?

Suppose that our 'laws of nature' were mere anomalies! Suppose that our planet Earth was a statistical variation, and the rest of the universe operated on totally different principles!

My imagination was being drawn irresistibly down such paths as these, leading to who could tell what appalling conclusions, when I was prosaically interrupted by the arrival of the breakfast I had ordered, and the capsules of forced-sleep drug.

I was so relieved to be distracted from my gloomy musings that I tipped the girl who brought the breakfast with absurd generosity. I poured a full cup of scalding black coffee, gulped it down, and followed it with another. My raging thoughts began to stabilize. I told myself that it was no good speculating about the future — I'd had most of my assumptions reduced to nonsense. I would be far better advised to wait until I'd satisfied myself that Leon was really and truly in this monstrous form he was alleged to have acquired. I wasn't looking forward to the experience, but at least it offered me escape from this limbo of uncertainty.

Meantime . . . Carmen.

There was little I could do where she was concerned. In the two and a half hours before the staff car which Suvorov had promised came to fetch me to the spaceport, I had to get at least the full hour of forced-sleep he'd insisted on. I dared not lose the opportunity of going up to *Starventure* even though I wasn't going to be allowed to write anything about what I saw on the trip. The space-service doctors would certainly refuse to allow me aboard the ferry if I was dropping with weariness; I had previous knowledge of the thoroughness with which they screened passengers going up to orbit. And in any case it seemed that the psychologists up there at the ship were depending on my encounter with Leon for valuable fresh information. It would be unfair to go up in less than peak physical condition.

Yet how I could face dropping off to sleep when I wanted most of all to brace myself, argue with myself, convince myself that I must trust these people who were making the ridiculous claim: *that thing in the many-legged body is your brother* . . . !

And also I wanted to be with Carmen.

Where could she have gone?

I considered asking Brian to trace her, on the specious excuse that he must want to obtain further details of her vision of her brother. But right now I had no idea how to contact Brian except by leaving a message which he might get while I was too deeply asleep to answer his call. He might be at the spaceport, or at Chambord's office, or anywhere; he might in fact already have started going round to call on the people from whom he'd heard rumours about the appearance of *Starventure's* crew in Quito.

I comforted myself with the thought that logically he would be looking for Carmen along with everyone else. And it might, I reasoned, be better if he found her without my prompting. Last night she had said to me, 'You don't own me.'

Which had suddenly made it clear that I wanted to. The next thing I intended to say to Señorita Carmen Iglesias was: 'Will you marry me?' In the terrible new universe I saw looming before me I desperately wanted to have and keep someone like her, who was not utterly committed to the falsehoods of an arbitrary and outmoded 'reality'.

Suppose an ant, immensely proud of her race's vast public works, mastery of building techniques, and the art of farming and domesticating other insects, were suddenly to become aware of the existence of man: she would feel very much as I felt now.

I had been picking at my breakfast while thinking along these lines. Abruptly I could endure it no longer. I pushed back my plate, picked up the forced-sleep capsules, and went to fetch a glass of water to wash them down.

After forced-sleep, at least one could not remember what one had dreamed.

It had struck me belatedly that leaving my hotel in broad daylight in a UN car was apt to wreck my chances of persuading people I'd gone down to Chile for a day or two. Fortunately the same point must have occurred to Suvorov; the car he sent had no insignia and the driver wasn't wearing uniform. He was a taciturn local man whose Indian ancestry showed in his long solemn face.

It was already possible to sense the effect of the release about *Starventure* this morning. There was an indefinable aura of gloom over the city. The municipal banners were still up in the streets, against the time of the heroes' welcome which had been planned for the crew, but people were pretending not to notice them as they walked below. And at the point where the road to the spaceport branched off the highway, there was something new: a police checkpoint at which five or six cars were lined up while their drivers expostulated with the officials in charge. My driver flashed an authorization card and we were let through, the target of curious stares. I kept my head down and hoped no one would recognize me.

Either Suvorov hadn't found the necessary hour to spare for a dose of forced-sleep, or he'd taken the stuff three days running and passed the point at which it remained effective. I suspected the latter, because last night he had complained to Brandt about the noise we were making while he was trying to rest. On the fourth day one was supposed to have twelve hours' natural sleep to catch up, and he'd obviously not managed it.

I wasn't taken to his office, but to a conference room in the same block. There were about a dozen people present altogether, including Suvorov, whose ghastly drawn face was the first thing to strike me. Next to him was General Cassiano, a plump sallow Italian with a small moustache and Imperial beard; he was in overall command of the starship base, and I'd met him a couple of times during the launch preparations two years ago. I also recognized Lenister and a woman called Doris Quantrell whom I had once interviewed at Columbia when I was doing a book on recent developments in psychology. There was the woman whose conference Suvorov had interrupted for us last night, a man in space-service uniform whose collar bore the caduceus tags of the medical branch, and a number of others.

I had the immediate impression I'd walked into the middle of a violent argument. Cassiano's words confirmed that.

'Ah, Mr Drummond! We've met before, of course, haven't we? Take the chair at the end of the table, will you? We were just discussing the matter of this — ah — *invitation* which General Suvorov extended to you.'

I sat down as directed, looking from face to face around the oblong table which extended virtually the whole length of the room. I could tell pretty clearly, just by glancing at them, which of these people had been raising objections.

'Correction,' I said. 'The suggestion was mine, and I made it the price of my co-operation in concealing the facts about what's happened up at *Starventure*.'

Doris Quantrell stiffened and threw a venomous glare at Suvorov. He didn't notice. I imagined he was having to concentrate exclusively on staying awake.

'General Cassiano!' she snapped. 'We'd already agreed that this was all going to be kept secret! Nothing about it was to be revealed to the crew's families — least of all to a man who is also a reporter!'

'Doris, I've told you before, Lenister cut in. 'It isn't enough simply to keep our mouths shut. People are getting suspicious, and who can blame them for that? We were damned lucky that Drummond was available, and willing to help us out. He's not *just* Leon Drummond's brother, and he's not *just* a reporter — he's won the Kalinga Prize for science writing, and he has a reputation which will do a great deal to damp down these wild rumours which are flying around.'

'On that score I don't think there's much room for argument,' Cassiano said. 'If you'll permit me, I'll take your more technical objections later, Dr Quantrell. Meantime, may we hear from Major Kamensky?'

The man with the caduceus collar-tabs turned to me. 'Have you flown space before, Mr Drummond?'

'Yes, a couple of times,' I said. 'I have about a hundred hours' space experience altogether. The first time was about five years ago, just after my brother was hired to work on *Starventure*. The second was three years back, during the assembly of the hull.'

'Did you suffer any vertigo, nausea, bone softening or impairment of spatial orientation?'

'None at all.'

'And since you last flew space have you suffered from any serious injuries or diseases which required hospitalization or extensive medical treatment?'

'No, I've enjoyed excellent health.'

Kamensky glanced at Cassiano. 'I reserve the right to change my mind after I've had a chance to give Mr Drummond a proper examination, but at this stage I have no objection in principle to his flying space.'

'Good − thank you.' Cassiano shifted in his chair. 'Now let's hear from you, Dr Lenister. I gather you're strongly in favour of this proposal.'

'Definitely!' Lenister hunched forward, once again wiping his glasses − it seemed to be a nervous habit with him. 'I don't know what's got into Doris. If I hadn't been so desperately preoccupied, I'd have realized much sooner that we needed a convincing cover story to fool the public. I'm delighted with what Drummond and his colleague have done for us.'

'What's that got to do with it?' snapped Doris Quantrell. 'He may be hell with jets when it comes to journalism, but that's no reason to let him go up to *Starventure!* Suvorov damned well ought to have consulted us beforehand!'

Cassiano made to say something, but changed his mind and let Lenister answer direct.

'Then you just haven't been listening, Doris − that's all I can say. *I want data*, and so should you! I want information about what's going on in those minds! Drummond here is a close relative of one of the crew; he's had a scientific education; he's experienced in meeting strangers and assessing them, and communicating his reaction in writing or on tape. I want to know what happens when someone with this sort of background confronts a member of the crew.'

'You want! You want!' Dr Quantrell said scornfully. 'So I'll tell you what *I* want! I want to cure you of this absurd bee in your bonnet about "transfer of personality into another bodily form" − do I quote you correctly, *Doctor* Lenister? I want us to do something practical and constructive to protect ourselves against the alien monsters which are trying to use the blockheadedness of people like you as a Trojan horse for their attack on this planet!'

So that was what the real argument was about. Not about me at all, nor about Suvorov's unauthorized action. A chill of terror passed down my spine.

13

Suddenly Lenister lost control. His face turned beet-red, and he clamped his hands on the edge of the table so violently that I had wild visions of him breaking pieces out of the wood and crushing them to dust. For several seconds he was too choked with fury to speak. Then he forced out words aimed at Cassiano like bullets from a gun.

'Get rid of this goddamned woman! Get her off this project before I break her arrogant neck! She's so stuffed with phobias no one else around her can hope to get any work done! How the hell do you expect us to get what we want out of Drummond when she's deliberately setting out to bias his mind? I can't stand it a moment longer – I'm getting the hell out!'

He jumped to his feet so quickly that his chair overturned and crashed on the floor behind him, stormed towards the door, ignoring the attempts of Kamensky and others to intercept him, and went out cursing in a horrible subdued monotone.

There was a frozen pause. Everyone looked at Cassiano, on whose olive-sallow face beads of perspiration were standing out.

'I'm going to recess this conference for an hour,' he said at last. 'I can hardly call Dr Lenister's behaviour constructive, but on the other hand I feel as he does, Dr Quantrell, that you're deliberately trying to provoke him. Major Kamensky!'

The doctor looked up.

'Before we reassemble, I want you to administer tranquillizers to both Dr Quantrell and Dr Lenister. I'm making that a condition of their rejoining us – be quiet, Dr Quantrell!' he added sharply as he saw her framing an objection. 'I mean exactly what I say: you come back tranquillized or not at all! I am *sick* of your wrangling with Lenister. I am also sick of your childish insistence on getting your own way because of your sex.'

It was Dr Quantrell's turn to jump to her feet and march out. Nobody tried to stop her. There was another interval of silence. I looked at Suvorov; he had leaned back in his chair and closed his eyes, and I judged that his exhaustion had finally caught up with him.

I couldn't say I was greatly surprised by the scene I'd just witnessed. I'd had a hint of the emotional strain these people must be undergoing in my hotel room this morning. A solid week of that kind of pressure, and you'd expect the cracks to show.

The woman on whose meeting Suvorov had burst in last night, who was sitting on Kamensky's left and had not spoken since I came in, now stirred and made to catch Cassiano's eye. He said, 'Yes, Miss Tobolkin?'

Automatically my memory glossed the name: Tatiana Tobolkin, Institute of Aerobotany — that incredible place in Siberia where they had duplicated forty square miles of the surface of Mars so that Martian vegetables could be studied at leisure and Earthly plants could be adapted to the hostile environment. I'd always meant to visit it, and somehow never found the time.

'I'm opposed to any recess,' Miss Tobolkin said in strongly accented English. 'Dr Quantrell has wrecked the original idea. As I understand it, the intention was to find out whether Mr Drummond's spontaneous reaction to the creature we've identified as his brother supported Dr Lenister's view that we have a transfer of personality into another body, or Dr Quantrell's belief in malevolent alien invaders. We must make a decision in principle at once, and I wish to state that despite what has happened the proposed confrontation remains both desirable and useful. If Mr Drummond would now be prejudiced, then we must invite some other close relative of the crew with a sufficiently resilient personality to accept the shock.'

'Then we'll vote,' Cassiano said. 'We're still a quorum. Those who agree with Miss Tobolkin, please.'

Suvorov moved to put his right elbow on the table and raised his hand. It shook like a leaf in the wind. After a moment of hesitation Kamensky copied him, and so did all but two of the others.

'Very well,' Cassiano said. 'We make our decision now in spite of the absence of Doctors Quantrell and Lenister.'

'Oughtn't we to hear what Mr Drummond thinks?' Suvorov suggested in a hoarse voice. 'He comes fresh to the problem as of last night. We've been getting stale.'

'Agreed,' Cassiano nodded. 'Mr Drummond, does what's happened since you came in need any explanation, or is it quite plain what's been going on?'

I cleared my throat. The chill of terror was still upon me; I felt like a walking corpse.

I said, 'Well, you don't have to explain that there are two schools of thought here. Dr Lenister thinks the minds — the personalities — of the crew are still present in their altered bodies. I've been struggling with the idea ever since last night, and because I don't see any way this could be managed right now it seems to me just as reasonable to go along with Dr Quantrell.'

'Ah, but that involves the assumption that the aliens responsible have so deep an understanding of human psychology that they can adopt individual personality patterns.' As though hauling his voice up from a deep well, Suvorov raised the counter-argument. 'It's not consistent to argue that they would then have to present themselves to us in their own bodies.'

'That's Lenister's strongest point,' Cassiano said. 'It does seem logical to assume that imitating the physical shape of a man would be easier than imitating his personality. Yet — making allowances for the difficulty of communication — the psychologists who prepared the profiles of the crew before departure have one by one come round to the belief that there's been a real continuity of identity.'

I shook my head. 'I'm out of my depth,' I muttered. 'So before making up my mind, could I just ask one or two more questions?'

'One or two!' Cassiano snorted. 'You're very considerate, Mr Drummond. If I were you, I'd want to put one or two *thousand* questions!' He settled more comfortably in his chair and gestured for me to go ahead.

'Well, let's assume that these aliens have in fact made an exchange of bodies: what conceivable purpose could they have for doing it?'

85

The man facing Kamensky, a lean type with a lantern jaw, indicated his willingness to tackle that.

'I'm Joost van Camp, Mr Drummond — University of Leyden. I don't believe we've met. Ah . . .' He hesitated. 'Well, at present we're considering the idea that the stories of members of the starship crew being seen on Earth have a basis in fact; you're one of the people concerned, I gather. In that case, it would follow that the aliens have never noticed us before, and have as it were borrowed the bodies of the crew so that they can look our planet over at first hand.'

'Fair enough,' I nodded. 'But does this imply that they're benevolent or hostile?'

Dr van Camp spread his hands. 'What have we to go on? So far they haven't done us any harm — unless you count the psychological shock suffered by the crew. But this need not indicate that they're well disposed towards us; it may only indicate caution, stemming from ignorance of our capabilities relative to their own.'

'Are the crew' — I hunted for another word, but couldn't find one, and the others were waiting for me — 'satisfied with the bodies they've been given?'

Miss Tobolkin leaned forward. 'This is what's so extraordinary,' she said. 'It seems that they are. In fact, making allowance for our ignorance of any kind of biology bar Terran and Martian, I'd be prepared to say that the bodies have been specially constructed to make the occupants comfortable.'

'Constructed?' I echoed in astonishment. 'You mean they aren't organic?'

'Organic, of course!' She made an impatient gesture. 'But they have several traits which suggest artificiality.'

'For instance?'

'You know, I imagine, that these creatures aboard *Starventure* breathe oxygen and exhale CO_2, can eat normal food with some extra trace elements, and drink water — in prodigious quantities, by the way. But all the trace elements we've so far tracked through the metabolism appear to be required in order to provide faculties superior to the human. In particular the nerve tissue, including the eyes which can see much further into the short end of the spectrum than we can, demands about ninety per cent of the unusual substances we've listed. Without going into exces

86

sive detail, I feel we must be dealing with the end product of a modification from a starting point rooted in a biology quite different from any we're familiar with.'

'Even more crucial,' put in van Camp, 'is the absence of a reproductive system.'

Miss Tobolkin gave a vigorous nod of agreement.

'Dr van Camp,' I said when I'd digested the last remarks, 'are you assuming that — if the crew's minds are in alien bodies — there are alien minds in the crew's bodies, correspondingly, walking around here on Earth?'

'If you can come up with a better working hypothesis,' he answered in an unhappy voice, 'we'd be delighted to learn of it.'

'Could these creatures possibly come from the Alpha Centauri system?'

'No.' Miss Tobolkin gave the word great emphasis. 'Not unless every record aboard the ship has been falsified — which admittedly isn't impossible. Landings were made just as we announced to the public, on two small planets and a number of satellites and asteroids, and all of them were found to be barren. One of the planets will probably develop life in a few million years because it has large pools of oily carbon-based compounds, but there's naturally no free oxygen and it's further from its sun than Mars.'

'Then where the hell do they come from? Hyperspace?'

'We're still arguing about that,' van Camp shrugged. 'It has been suggested. I don't pretend to follow the reasoning, because this isn't my field, but apparently it can be shown mathematically that our space might prove to be a variant of a greater space, and the latter ought to permit the kind of energy processes which life depends on. It might even be a more efficient setting for life.'

More efficient, maybe . . . but *weird*! I prevented myself from letting my mind wander off down an unprofitable avenue of speculation, and went on with my questions.

'When I was shown that picture of — well, of my *brother* last night, at first glance I thought it was a photo of a sky-monster. Are you assuming that the apparitions in the sky indicate that the aliens are looking out of their own universe into ours?'

'Well, there is a remarkable resemblance in general body structure between the sky-monsters and the present shape of the crew,' van Camp agreed.

'But in that case the creatures must be colossal!' My nape prickled. 'How big are the ones aboard the ship?'

'About the mass of a man,' Miss Tobolkin said crisply. 'Their average weight is sixty-three kilos.'

During the past few exchanges Cassiano had been showing signs of mounting impatience. Now he seized the chance to break in and address me.

'Mr Drummond, forgive me for cutting you short, but right now we do have to reach a decision. Let me ask you straight out: on the basis of what you've been told, are you still prepared to act as a guinea pig for us — to confront the creature we suspect of being your brother Leon?'

'Yes,' I said, as steadily as I could. I wasn't looking forward to the experience, but I was determined to go.

'And do you think you've heard enough of both sides of the argument to keep an open mind up till the actual meeting?'

'I can't honestly answer that,' I said after a pause. 'But I will try.'

Cassiano gave a grunt and looked around the table. 'At present,' he reminded his audience, 'we're empowered to act on our own discretion. It's possible that this state of affairs won't last, and in any case however things turn out we shall almost certainly have to justify ourselves before a UN committee of inquiry. I'd like you to bear that in mind when you vote.'

After a pause to let the point sink in, he took the vote and it was unanimously in favour of letting me go up to the starship.

'Good, thank you. Mr Drummond, would you go with Major Kamensky, then? We only have one launch scheduled for today, at 1650 hours, but your medical check and kitting out must be complete by 1500 at the latest.'

Except for Suvorov, who had given up the struggle to stay awake and now slumped snoring in his chair, the others were rising to their feet with expressions of relief.

'And — good luck!' Cassiano said. 'If that means anything any more.'

I nodded and made blindly for the door in Kamensky's wake. I was trying to decide which would be worse: to find my brother trapped in a monstrous body, or a monster masquerading as my brother.

Both possibilities struck me as equally horrible.

14

They'd developed some new wrinkles since I last underwent a pre-space medicheck. The sugar booster injection into the liver no longer left behind a feeling like a day-old bruise, and that was good, but they were giving the decelerine-cum-antinausea shot — all thirty cc's of it — into the gluteus maximus instead of intravenously, and that was bad; it made me feel as though I'd been bitten by a mosquito two inches too far under the skin to scratch the spot. I asked Kamensky the reason, and he said the drugs had to be allowed to diffuse more slowly since the introduction of the modern slow-burning ferry fuels, which kept down the total *g* forces but greatly lengthened the time to *brennschluss*.

Otherwise the process was familiar. Apart from having gone through it twice before myself, I'd watched it on a dozen occasions and written it up nearly as often. Moreover, Kamensky's staff were a very smooth-working team. At first, I think, they were worried about me — having had trouble, I gather, with some of the scientific high brass they'd had to process recently; people desperately needed up in orbit yet by all normal standards not healthy enough to stand the strain. But I keep myself in good physical shape, and when I went back into Kamensky's office at the end of the check to learn the verdict, I found him smiling.

'I wish all our special passengers posed as few problems as you do, Mr Drummond,' he said as he ran his eyes over the final report. 'Your B-12 is down a little, so I've marked you for an oral supplement — and incidentally you should have that checked by your own doctor when you get back — but otherwise you're almost up to the standard we demand of our pilots. Now how about food? Can you take a pre-space dry meal, or would you rather have a glucose shot and wait till you're in orbit before you eat again?'

'No, I've had dry meals both times before.'

'More than I can manage,' Kamensky grunted. 'To me they taste like compressed sawdust, and I don't care how nutritious they may be. But it is certainly better to go up with your guts working on something, so you can collect one from the canteen on your way to be kitted out. Don't drink anything before takeoff, though, will you? If you need to moisten your mouth after the meal, take a one cc cube of ice at the latest possible moment. And you know about emptying your bladder and bowels before strapdown. That's the lot, then.'

He got up and stretched his hand across his desk.

'I'll repeat what General Cassiano said – good luck. But I share his view that this probably doesn't mean much any more.'

Medically inspected, fed, kitted out, I emerged into the pre-space briefing room. I'd taken the ice after my dry meal, but the permitted size of the lump was smaller than the end of my little finger, and I felt as though I'd just walked across the Sahara.

The room was dominated by a huge internally illuminated orrery showing the Earth, the Moon and everything in orbit around those two bodies. Over the course of the past half century, the number had reached a respectable total. At present the mechanism was set to show apparent relative motion from a fixed point in space, and it took me only a moment to figure out that the reference was *Starventure*.

A group of three people stood before the orrery's airtight case talking in low tones. Cassiano was in the middle; on his right was a stranger in well-worn spacekit who barely came to his elbow – a pilot, I guessed, knowing that physical slightness was at a premium in that job. And on his left, looking morose, was Lenister.

They turned at my approach. I saw the pilot's face for the first time, and checked in midstride. The face was Chinese or Japanese, finely formed with large luminous eyes, but that wasn't what surprised me. It was the red of the lips. I was perfectly aware that many of the leading space pilots were women, but this was the first time I'd encountered a woman pilot in context.

Cassiano greeted me and introduced me to the pilot, whose name proved to be Becky Koo. She shook my hand with a firm grip.

'Glad to meet you, Mr Drummond,' she said in excellent

English. 'I know your books, of course — in fact I rely on them to keep me in touch with fields I don't have time to study thoroughly.'

I muttered something about being flattered.

'You'd better get kitted out, Dr Lenister,' Cassiano went on. 'It's nearly 1500, and you ought to be going aboard.'

'Lord! So it is!' Lenister exclaimed with a glance at his watch. 'Right, I'll be as quick as I can.'

As he moved away, I asked a wondering question of Cassiano with my eyes, and he shrugged.

'Well, he's fit enough to fly space — Kamensky checked him out the day before yesterday — but we had to send up some urgent equipment instead by the ferry he was supposed to be taking. And he keeps complaining about having to judge by secondhand information, so . . .'

'Who else is up there already?' I demanded. 'I know more or less who's come out here to the port — the names read like *Who's Who in Science* — but I imagine some must have failed the medicheck.'

'Yes, that's one of our worst difficulties.' Cassiano wiped his forehead with a large green tissue. 'We have the world's finest minds to call on, but we can't put them into overhauled bodies.' He smiled a little at his sick joke. 'Dr Tobolkin wants to go up, and I'm sure she'd be valuable, but she has a weak heart, and Dr van Camp suffers from acute vertigo; he'd panic in a free-fall environment. But up at the ship we have all the experts we can muster, with the psychologists working under Graubmayer and Sico and the physiologists under Rokossovsky.'

That would be Ivan Pavlovitch Rokossovsky, Nobel Prize in medicine two years ago. I'd known that all three were in Quito; they were at the top of the list of people I'd been trying unsuccessfully to locate.

'Has everyone who's come to the port since *Starventure's* return either stayed here or gone up to orbit?' I asked.

'Pretty well,' Cassiano grunted. 'You couldn't say we have a shortage of talent. But a more temperamental, argumentative, *pigheaded* bunch you couldn't find anywhere!'

It seems to have almost the force of a law of nature that the faster the vehicle you want to travel in the longer you spend preparing for the journey. Twenty years after it had become possible to walk straight on board an inter-continental aircraft with no formalities apart from buying a ticket, here we were, an hour before lift-off, being told to make for our ferry.

Dutifully we set out – on foot, because someone had forgotten to recharge the batteries of the little electric trolley which normally would have carried us from the briefing room. I didn't mind; in fact, in my present state of mind I preferred to walk. Becky Koo went a little ahead of Lenister and myself, humming a Chinese pop song with curious unexpected intervals.

'How are you feeling, Drummond?' Lenister muttered when we had covered about half the distance.

'I have a belly full of butterflies,' I said. 'You?'

'Terrible.' He gave a harsh chuckle. 'I was just wishing I had the guts to turn round and walk right back indoors. I've never flown space before, you know. You said you had a hundred hours' experience, I think.'

I nodded.

'Wish I'd been up already,' he sighed. 'Kamensky filled me up with gallons of tranquillizer, but I'm still shaking all over . . . And I'm not even going to see a close relative in his – ah – *altered form*. How the hell can you be so calm in face of that?'

It was a good question. I thought for a while before answering. I said at length, 'Well, maybe I haven't made myself accept the idea on the emotional level. Maybe I'm subconsciously certain that when I get up there I'll find Leon looking and acting like his old self.'

'No, I'm afraid you won't. For a whole week, damned near, I've had to listen to Graubmayer on the radio, des-cribing his findings, and . . . you know how he talks, in a voice that's all thick, like cold porridge?'

'I've heard him at scientific congresses. I know what you mean.'

'Well, it's not the pictures they've sent down – the photos and the tight-beam TV transmissions. They look just plain unconvincing, like model shots. But hearing stolid old Graubmayer soberly listing these utterly incre-dible results he's got – that's what really shakes the mind.' He chuckled again, with nervousness this time. 'By the way, I ought to apologize to you, shouldn't I? I mean, for blasting off at Doris Quantrell this morning.'

'No need,' I said. 'You've all been under terrible stress this past week, and there's no sign of it being over.'

'Yes, but Doris is the last straw! Have you met her before?'

'Yes, I interviewed her for my syndicated science column.'

'I met her here for the first time. I've been at the Sorbonne for several years, of course, and though I think we've attended the same congress a couple of times I never actually talked to her there. I find her absolutely insufferable. I'm not usually prejudiced against women, but after what Doris has done to me lately I'm not even very happy about going into space with a woman pilot!'

'Has she applied to go up to *Starventure*?'

'Yes, but Kamensky vetoed the application, thank God. He wasn't going to tell her why, but she insisted, and finally he lost his temper and told her straight out she's a hysteric and he wasn't going to answer for the consequences if she was allowed aboard a spaceship. Naturally, when Kamensky proceeded to pass me as fit, her dislike of me turned to actual hatred – and you saw some of the effects of that this morning.'

I nodded, but didn't answer. I was suddenly distracted by the terrifying vision of all the petty personal feuds and irritations which stood between us and a rational solution to this mystery.

The ground crew had finished loading the crates of equipment which the ferry was taking up in its hold. Now their balloon-tyred vehicles were backing away from the sleek Wallis-winged form of the ship, and the crew escalator was being eased towards the airlock. I was disappointed at having to wait even for a couple of minutes, and passed the time in noting the minor design improvements they'd adopted since I was last this close to a space ferry, two years ago.

Like all the ferries operating out of Quito – and indeed 90 per cent of those in service anywhere on Earth – this was an RRR: rocket-ramjet-rocket. The nose now was slanted at seventy degrees above the horizontal, and the longitudinal axis of course was aligned parallel to the equator. On either side of the tail there stuck out tubby shapes like coke bottles – the kickpots, which in one flaming burst would hurl the ship through the dense lower layers of the atmosphere. At ninety thousand feet, with Mach 6 showing on the instrument board, they would reach *brennschluss* and detach themselves; they would fall thirty thousand feet and then a thermite charge would ignite to ensure they never returned to the surface except as dust. Meantime, the single huge ramjet around which the hull of the ship was assembled would come into operation; the nose-cone would be blown off, to suffer the same fate as the kickpots, and with a scream too soft to be heard in the thin upper air the energy from ozone and free radicals would whip the vessel clear to orbital velocity. When the air became too thin for the ramjet, pure rockets would serve to make our rendezvous with *Starventure*.

'I never realized these things were so big!' Lenister exclaimed as we awaited the okay signal from the man steering the escalator into position.

'This is the S-class ferry,' I said. 'About two hundred and seventy feet overall. Weight about a thousand tons without the kickpots.'

'Fantastic.' He stared up, craning his neck, towards the distant nosecone.

Normally I'd have been more forthcoming, given him as long a rundown on the technical data as he could stand. It was part of my stock in trade to feel excitement about our ingenuity and communicate it on paper. But right now . . .

'How do they land them? I've been here a week and I never had time to watch it done.'

'I'm sorry — what?'

Lenister repeated his question, and I said, 'Oh, it's fitted with Wallis wings. Variable configuration. It glides back down, losing speed against the rotation of the Earth, and makes its approach at about four hundred miles an hour. Then it gets a signal from the ground which fires the forward rockets — you can just see the nozzles, but they've got fairings over them, of course. And the same signal triggers the wings into the drag position. It has to be done automatically because the exhaust from the forward rockets completely covers the ship. Don't try watching a landing without dark glasses; all you can see is a red-hot ball of gas diving on to the port. It touches down on retractable skids at about a hundred and twenty and brakes to a dead stop in less than a mile.'

'Sounds uncomfortable.' He tried to smile, but the effect was ghastly.

'No, in fact it isn't provided your pilot sets up a really accurate approach, so ground control doesn't have to make any sudden course adjustments, and these things touch down as smoothly as a civil airliner.'

'Well, I'll be damned,' Lenister said, his eyes wandering back to the dominating bulk of the ship. 'I hadn't realized they'd brought space travel down to such a fine art.'

I finished what I'd been telling myself when he interrupted my train of thought. I'd been reflecting that whereas I was usually enthusiastic about our own cleverness, right now I was apparently faced with creatures who could not only 'borrow' human bodies and 'lend' others of their own making to the displaced proprietors, but could then place those bodies on Earth's surface zephyr-gently, without benefit of ships, or rockets, or a spaceport like this one.

I recalled my conceited ant, who had just found out about human beings.

15

One thing nobody had warned me about was the smell. It hit me the instant I cracked my suit on the in-ship side of *Starventure's* personnel lock. It wasn't the submarine staleness of air used and re-used past the ability of the conditioners to cleanse it, though that was there too. It was an alien smell: a hint of ammonia, of formaldehyde, of incompletely oxydized fats, plus too many other things for my nose to analyze.

Lenister, very pale and clinging to the straps on the bulkhead as though afraid to cast off into free fall, noticed it a moment after I did.

'Like a zoo!' he exclaimed.

But that wasn't quite right. It hadn't been our decision to bring strange creatures here and pen them up.

'You mean the stink?' said the girl who had been waiting to see us through the lock. She looked and sounded West

95

African, but she hadn't offered to introduce herself. 'Oh, you'll get used to it in an hour or two. Which of you is Dr Lenister?'

'I am,' Lenister said, still clinging with one hand. In the other he clutched his helmet while glancing about him for somewhere to put it. The girl solved his problem by taking it and tossing it at a magnetized panel, where it landed with a click.

'Professor Graubmayer asked for you to be brought to him directly on arrival,' she said. 'This way, please.'

She eeled through the inner door of the lock with a quick swimming motion and set off along the corridor beyond. As best we could − I'd never had time to learn the knack of gravity-less running, and Lenister had never attempted it before − we followed her.

There was almost the feel of a space-borne city about *Starventure*; compared to any other spaceship we had ever built she was as an ocean liner to an aircraft. You could have put two of the regular Mars ships inside her hull and left room for an orbital ferry as well. I'd studied her design pretty closely when writing up the story of her departure for the stars, but that wasn't much help in locating where we were right now. The brief glimpse we'd had while transferring from the ferry hadn't told me which of four possible locks we were being taken through nor which way her nose was pointed. From the curvature of the corridor I guessed we might be heading in the midships direction.

I was wrong. The door before which our guide brought herself to a halt long enough to activate the lock was labelled FORWARD FERRY HOLD. Beyond, there should have been a huge compartment into which the ferry could be drawn by a set of enormous hydraulic waldos. There wasn't. Or rather, the hold was still there, but it had been converted to other uses.

What they had done, I later learned, was to push the ferry out into space and couple it up to one of the after locks − because any habitable space was currently at a premium up here and people could sleep and eat in the ferry − and divide up the empty hold with lightweight screens. Into the boxlike rooms so created they'd tossed computers, scientific instruments, crates of microfilm and magnetape, and inevitably scientists. It was eerie to see an Elliott Million computer upside-down directly beyond the door, not resting on a stand but simply tethered, its power cable looping like a drunken snake across its back.

I heard Lenister gulp as the man working at the computer, hanging head-down in relation to ourselves, glanced our way and spoke. It was Graubmayer himself, and his voice was indeed like curdled porridge.

'Glad you made it, Lenister. Is that Drummond you've brought with you? And turn over so I can talk to you the right way up!'

The girl pulled back to the wall of the corridor to let us past, then closed the door of the hold and abandoned us. We rolled over to the same attitude as Graubmayer, and found things a little better that way up.

'Welcome to aboriginal chaos,' he went on with a trace of bitterness. 'I'm trying to get a print-out of our findings so far about Leon Drummond, but some double-dyed idiot put a wrong address on part of the data, and I can't locate them in the memory.'

'Siegfried!' a shrill voice called from the other side of the nearest partition. 'Try punching for continuity of personality — you should be able to work out the right address from that!'

'That's what I'm doing, thanks,' Graubmayer called back. 'Just waiting for it to print out now.'

I noticed that a piece of mesh had been glued over the delivery vent of the computer to stop the tape flying out and getting tangled. As I glanced towards it, the little red light signifying DATA ORGANIZED began to blink, and the tape emerged.

Graubmayer gave a sigh. 'So at last we have what we're after — but I should have had it an hour ago!' He eased a yard or two of the tape out of the slot and studied it as he went on, 'Now you're Leon Drummond's brother; isn't that right?'

Carelessly, I nodded, and as a result began to rock back and forth in mid air.

'I heard from the base that you'd volunteered to come up here, and personally I'm very grateful. I wouldn't care to go through it myself in cold blood. It's bad enough being slightly acquainted with members of the crew — I knew Chandra Dan, for example, who spent a while teaching at the same university as myself. But I've studied your brother's pre-flight personality charts, and I gather that you and he were even closer than siblings usually are, as a result of being orphaned.'

'Where —' My voice failed me; I had to swallow and start again. 'Where is he?'

'Oh, we've left the crew in their own quarters. We've disturbed the routine they established during the trip as little as we possibly could. Anything which tends to stabilize the environment, of course, helps to normalize their behaviour. And we've merely cleared out the two ferries, which were used for storing records on the way home anyway. You probably saw them orbiting alongside as you came in.'

'No,' Lenister said. 'We didn't see a damned thing.' He tried a laugh.

'How soon can I see Leon?' I pressed. Now I was actually here, now the moment was upon me, waiting seemed unendurable.

'As soon as we can arrange it!' Graubmayer snapped, suddenly revealing that he too was being worn out by the strain, as Suvorov was, and Lenister — indeed, everyone concerned.

Lenister cleared his throat. 'I think we ought to hurry,' he ventured. 'We're only supposed to be up here for twenty-four hours, and if possible I feel we should confront Mr Drummond with his brother two or three times.'

'We're not dragging our feet, Lenister!' Graubmayer retorted.

I pulled myself back to the bulkhead and waited with as much patience as I could contrive. Listening as Lenister and Graubmayer talked, to each other and to people who appeared from elsewhere in the hold to ask advice or report recent findings, I supplemented what I already knew from Suvorov.

The physical change — assuming that was what had happened — might have taken place earlier than Suvorov had said. The crew had got into the habit of going naked, which wasn't surprising; the crew of Mars vessels seldom wore more than trunks, because skin was easier to keep clean aboard a spaceship than clothing. Consequently getting dressed could not have offered a clue to what had occurred, and it might have been as long as a month before the unfortunates who went to break out spacesuits were suddenly forced into awareness of their plight. Up until that moment they'd had no inkling. The curious blind spot which had been created in each mind was one of the most puzzling aspects of the whole affair.

Suvorov had said the 'new bodies' weren't equipped for talking. That wasn't strictly true. Some or all of the bodies could generate and detect sounds beyond the normal range, rather higher than a bat's squeak. Sound-converters had been brought up a couple of days ago — I got the impression that that was the cargo which had taken precedence over Lenister — and more had come up by our own ferry, so it was becoming possible to conduct conversations.

That disposed of an inconsistency which had earlier troubled me. I'd been told that some of the crew had attempted to greet the boarding party who discovered them, which would not have been possible if they'd suddenly realized they had no power of speech. It left another: why, if they were able to talk at all, they had continued to transmit code-groups instead of using radio when they came in range.

The talk passed out of my area of comprehension after that. I'd always kept well abreast of the physical sciences, including fringe disciplines like aerobotany and spatio-chemistry, but I was some years behind with the latest developments in psychology — as I'd discovered from working on a book which I'd started a year ago and still hadn't delivered to my angry publisher. Here they were talking about Duxman's Factor, and the *phi* quotient, and the variation curve of determinant scan, and I had only the haziest notion what the terms implied.

A girl came swimming around the hold with a net bag full of squeezebulbs of lukewarm coffee and gave one to each of us. Rokossovsky came from the after ferry hold where he was working on the physiological aspects of the problem to discuss a thorny point with Graubmayer; he was told who I was, gave me a smile, and forgot me again. Alvarez Sico, a lean, handsome Mexican with distinguished grey hair whom I'd met briefly at an international congress the way I'd met most of the world's scientific notables, was called to advise on some tactical question regarding my interview with Leon. Gradually ideas crystallized into plans.

At last Graubmayer turned and beckoned me over.

'We've run into a dilemma,' he admitted. 'We want the conditions for the meeting with your brother to be as ordinary as possible, but at the same time we want to extract the maximum amount of information from it. We'd like you to go to his cabin as though everything was perfectly normal, and just knock on the door and walk in, but we can't. We're going to have to bring you both to one of the large public rooms, where we'll have space to install our equipment. Sico here would like to festoon you with wires and terminals, but I've put my foot down and we've agreed to compromise on four recorders covering each of you. If you have no objection, I'll be present in person, and Lenister and Sico will watch over closed-circuit TV. And then afterwards, of course, we'll compare the records with what we've collected from our spy-eyes in the crew's quarters to see if we can detect any discrepancies in your – uh – alleged brother's behaviour. There is, of course, the vanishingly small chance that we're dealing with aliens pretending to have human minds, but if that's so we might as well quit here and now. A psychology like that would be totally beyond our comprehension.'

I felt a terrible wavering apprehension. 'How soon will you be ready?' I demanded.

'We'll set up the preparations right away,' Lenister shrugged. 'Graubmayer, where do you think would be most suitable?'

'It'll have to be the exercise hall,' Graubmayer answered. 'It's rather a stark setting, but we've used it for most of our physical and psychological tests so far, and there are enough power points to drive the sound-converter as well as all our recorders. You did gather, didn't you, Mr Drummond, that we expect your brother to be able to talk to you directly?'

'Yes.'

'Good. Then come this way.'

There was more waiting to endure when we reached the exercise hall, a bare room with all the bulkheads heavily padded so that free-fall games could be played in it. The exercise equipment on which every crewman had to spend at least half an hour a day to maintain muscle tone had been cleared away, and technicians were busy with the newly delivered sound-converters as well as wide-angle visual recorders and a great deal of other equipment. On spotting Graubmayer, one of the technicians called him over, and there was much discussion round a tapedeck from which issued a noise like the grunting of a herd of pigs. Abruptly I recognized it as a vastly distorted version of 'Mary Had a Little Lamb'. Apparently this confirmed Graubmayer's optimism about being able to talk to Leon directly, and when he returned to me he was rubbing his hands.

'We're ready to send for your brother now, Mr Drummond,' he said. 'I haven't made any particular suggestions about what you should say to him, and I don't propose to. I'm assuming that you can imagine situations that are at least analogous — long separation and physical disfigurement, for instance — where you'd need to satisfy yourself of the identity of someone claiming to be your brother. So I'll only request that so long as you have the least suspicion that the claim is false you control yourself and act naturally. We'll interrupt after an hour if you've not broken the interview off yourself before then.'

I felt myself shiver.

'Would you put this on, Mr Drummond?'

One of the technicians was offering me an earphone on a long elastic flex. I took it, glanced to see what it was connected to, and saw that it ran back to the bank of sound-converters. Dutifully I put it on.

'Don't expect to hear his own voice,' Graubmayer warned me. 'There may not be any resemblance at all after the frequencies have been stepped down so drastically. But the engineers have assured me they'll preserve every clue they can.'

'Yes, I appreciate that,' I said.

'Good. Lenister, will you and Sico go to the TV monitor? And the rest of you — out, as soon as you can!'

The hall emptied. Hanging on air, just out of arm's reach of Graubmayer, in a silence dominated by the pounding of my heart, I awaited the arrival of Leon — monster — Drummond.

16

Perhaps, if I hadn't been so numb with shock when Suvorov
showed me that photograph (less than twenty-four hours
ago! — was it possible?), I'd have been prepared for my
own reaction when the door of the exercise hall next slid
back. But I hadn't studied the picture closely; I'd retained
from it only a vague impression of misshapen horror, and
the memory had rapidly become muddled with the more
vivid image of the monster that had looked down on
Quito.

It was the grace of its movements that startled me. I
hadn't wondered how such a creature would look when it
moved. And while that surprise still had a hold on me, I
found myself thinking, 'Why — it's rather a handsome
beast!'

Black, with a kind of glistening cobalt sheen which
reminded me of the carapace of a tropical beetle, it drew
itself through the doorway with rhythmical motions of its
many legs. How many? I counted six, again reminiscent of
a beetle. But the overall effect was somehow not insectlike.
More, it resembled the gait of a moon-walker, the superbly
efficient machines they developed for long-distance trans-
port across the rocky lunar surface. Yes: certainly like a
well-designed machine. As the curious form came further
into the room, somehow shyly, I could see how neatly the
limbs were articulated on the body, how their leverage was
obtained, how even in the absence of gravity they suggested considerable strength without excessive bulk.

I thought of what Tatiana Tobolkin had said about the
possibility that these bodies might be artificial. If that body
was an artifact, the artificer was a genius.

There were eyes, not exactly set on a head . . . but then,
the mass to which the legs were attached wasn't precisely a
body, either. One might say 'thorax', but that again referred to insects and this wasn't an insect. I told myself to
say 'torso'. The eyes were different from those of the Quito
sky-monster, and I was somehow taken aback by the fact

Apart from their colour — a rich bluish green — they were quite like terrestrial eyes, having black pupils and mobile lids. But peculiar fringes of tendrils, hanging from below the eyes and from the forward edge of each limb, concealed many of the surface details. The tendrils were soft, and of a lighter colour than the rest. Otherwise the blue-blackness was uniform.

This creature, with as many legs as an insect, a machine-like precision of movement, and some additional quality which was wholly strange to me, checked itself by catching at the edge of the doorway with a hind limb. In my ear a voice which was not Leon's at all as regards timbre but entirely his as regards inflection and emphasis, spoke.

'For heaven's sake — Big Brother himself!'

I was so nervous I feared my voice would break, but it held out. I cracked back, remembering Graubmayer's injunction to behave as naturally as possible, 'What the hell have you been doing to yourself? I've never seen you in such lousy shape!'

He kicked free of the doorway and came closer, checking his flight with a precisely timed touch on one of the pieces of equipment fastened to the — well, floor.

'Obviously they warned you what to expect,' he said soberly. 'Nobody tells us anything; I didn't even know it was you waiting to see me until I reached the door there . . . Did they show you pictures?'

I nodded.

'It's the most extraordinary, incredible, impossible thing!' He jerked his front limbs so that the tips clicked together. In a human body he would have pounded his right fist into his left palm, a habit of Leon's whenever he was worked up about something. 'You heard it was done so cleverly that we didn't realize we'd been changed until the men from the tug came aboard and gave us a standard of visual comparison?'

'They told me that, but I don't see how it's possible. Surely you must — must *feel* different?'

'No, not at all, and that's the craziest part.' The voice in my earphone was earnest, almost pleading. 'Look, I have an extra pair of limbs. Up here in my head I'm aware of the fact, I look at you or Graubmayer and I count and I realize the difference. Yet I can't feel a discontinuity between my old body and my present one! These middle limbs' — he gestured with them — 'are either legs or arms according to the need of the moment, and they blend into my old memories so smoothly that I'm sometimes puzzled, thinking back, to remember that I sometimes had fiddling jobs to do when the extra hands would have been an advantage. I have to remind myself that there was a time when they weren't there.'

He broke off. 'Dave, I can recognize your expression. You're trying to pretend there's nothing bothering you. Well, there is, damn it! Your eyes tell you there isn't anything in common between this — this *object* in front of you and the Leon you used to know. Am I right?'

'You know you're right,' I said.

He made a helpless movement; it couldn't be a shrug because his shoulders weren't constructed for shrugging, but it conveyed the same message. 'I don't blame you for being sceptical. Directly after the men from the tug showed up, when we first realized what had happened, some of us went half out of our minds thinking that people would — well, shoot first and ask questions afterwards. Well, at least you've given us the benefit of the doubt. Crying was one of the things left out of these bodies, or we'd have drowned ourselves in an Alice pool from sheer relief. But now, of course, what's driving us nutty is trying to think of a way to make you believe down to the gut-level that we are who we think we are.'

I glanced at Graubmayer. He had withdrawn to a polite distance, about ten feet, and there was no trace of expression on his granite face.

'Did you meet, or see, the creatures responsible for your changing?' I ventured.

'Not that we knew of at the time. I suppose it's likely that we've seen them since then.' And, when I looked blank, he added, 'Sort of in silhouette, etched on the black of the sky. Don't they show up from the surface of Earth?'

Nobody had told me there had been any sky-monsters observed from orbit. I said as much, and he gave a laugh which came over remarkably human via the sound-converter.

'You have the same trouble we have, hm? People don't tell you things! It's the weirdest feeling, you know, to watch one of those, and remember that that's now a picture of yourself!'

'Mahee!' I said. Out of the corner of my eye, I saw

104

Graubmayer turn in astonishment. My monster-brother was quicker.

'Ma*hi*!' he exclaimed.

'Ma*ho*!' I capped, and we continued in chorus.

'Ma-rump-si pommadiddle mitkat nitkat heebo ibo wallahwallah cheesecake!'

A pause; then a chuckle. 'Good grief, I'd almost forgotten that. I can't have been more than six when you taught me to recite that bit of nonsense.'

'About that,' I said carefully. 'Wasn't it on the swing at the Fairwood house, the one under the apple tree?'

'No, surely not! We didn't have a swing at Fairwood. We had an apple tree, but it wasn't the one with the swing. That was a Posquahannet – don't you remember, the gulls used to come into the garden when there was a gale out at sea?'

I remembered perfectly well. And the fact that he did too told me not a damned thing.

Almost as though he'd read my thoughts, he said with a trace of bitterness, 'Not a bad try, Dave. But it's no use. I remember everything I remembered in my old body, as far as I and all the psychologists can discover. And the hell of it is, I feel so completely goddamned *normal* now! Of course, for a while I was pretty mixed up, as who wouldn't be after having this happen to him? But I wasn't nearly as badly hit as Chandra Dan. Did they tell you about him – how they had to process everything they said to him through a computer, because he couldn't latch on to the ordinary progress of time?'

I nodded. I couldn't trust myself to speak.

'But even he's recovered now. I was chatting with him myself just a short while back.'

Desperately I struggled to think of some indisputable proof of his identity. Previously I'd got no further in my analysis of the problem than childhood memories; after all, a person is the sum of consciously and unconsciously remembered experience. But if that ground had already been covered to no purpose . . .

'Ah – tell me something about the trip,' I said at random and felt the germ of a fresh idea sprout from the words. 'I don't mean the "we went and took a look and came back" stuff – I've had all that. But how your predictions about the subjective effects of the drive turned out, for example. You were very excited about that when you left.'

'Not half as excited as you were about Hermanos Iglesias's sister,' he countered dryly, 'Poor Hermanos is one of the worst affected of us, of course, because he has this big thing about family ties. He got pretty homesick, and he's not taking kindly to being cooped up here in the ship now the trip is over. Can I tell him that his sister is okay? What's her name — Carmen, isn't it?'

'Well, yes,' I said. 'As far as I know she's all right.'

'Does she know about — about *us*?'

I hesitated, but there was no point in lying. I gave a miserable nod.

'Poor girl! If she's anything like Hermanos, she's taking it a hell of a sight worse than you are, you cold fish. Have you spoken to her lately?'

'Last night — uh — I mean about twenty hours ago.' My tone of voice gave away more of my feelings than I'd intended.

'Well, well, it sounds as though you never got over her!' He chuckled. 'Lone Wolf Dave finally got his! Next you'll be telling me you're thinking about marriage.'

'As a matter of fact, I am,' I admitted. 'Though I don't know yet whether she is.'

'Well, I hope she says yes, and I hope you'll be very happy — as happy as anyone can be in our crazy new universe. But sex and marriage are kind of null subjects for us right now. What were we talking about when the gracious señorita walked on stage?'

'I was asking you a question,' I reminded him. Under the veneer of flippancy on his voice which survived even passage through the sound-converter, I thought I'd detected a note of repressed anger when he spoke of sex and marriage as 'null subjects', and that was a problem I felt could better be left to the psychologists; I was eager to get away from it.

'Ah yes: about the subjective effects of the drive.' He gave me a look which in human terms would have been a suspicious frown. 'You didn't go around quoting my ideas to everyone, did you? You didn't put them in one of your shiny-but-superficial books? Because it would be a hell of a note for me to have to back down on my guesses in public! Not a single prediction I made was borne out in practice. The ship stayed the ship, we stayed ourselves — up to the last minute,' he amended wryly. 'In short, our experience of hyperspace can be summed up by saying it's like ordinary space only rather more so. It's hard for me to explain it to someone who's never been there, but I can give you an idea of just how paradoxical the situation was by saying that it looks as though we're going to have to start treating our elaborate Einsteinian world-picture as a rather complicated special case of the traditional Euclidean one. There's a nice snippet of news for you to expound to your public! Before we left we were thinking of hyperspace as a peculiar "elsewhere" kind of phenomenon. From now on, I'm inclined to believe we must regard normal space as the "elsewhere". We just happen to have evolved in it. If you've done any homework on your *cis*-spatial maths since I've been away, maybe I can show you what I'm driving at. Dave, is something wrong?'

I must have been ghost-pale; certainly I was sweating all over and my hands were shaking. I couldn't make it clear how I'd come to my conclusion, but I had, and it felt positive.

I said, 'Hell, you *are* my brother. I don't see how you can be — but you're no one else in this cockeyed universe than Leon Drummond.'

17

After that they plagued me to explain: Graubmayer, Sico and Lenister by turns, separately or together. All I could say was that I had been convinced. Over and over I threw back what Graubmayer himself had said — that Leon and I had been even closer than most siblings; over and over I declared that I could have shut my eyes and forgotten it was a strange blue-black creature facing me.

The nearest I could come to defining what for me had settled the matter was to compare it with an author's style. Just as an experienced critic can tell by the flavour of a few paragraphs that they are the work of such and such a writer, I'd been compelled while listening to accept that Leon was talking. The turns of phrase were his, the little mannerisms of emphasis and hesitation could belong to nobody else.

Still they pestered me, until at last I could stand their interrogation no longer and blew up.

'For God's sake!' I shouted. 'What does it *mean* to go on asking whether this is really my brother? If there's some kind of super-being that can imitate him well enough to satisfy me, then by comparison we're nothing better than insects, and we'll have to learn to live with the fact!'

They exchanged frowns.

'I — I've been arguing on those lines,' Lenister said at last. 'But I can't get people to agree with me. Either their pride rebels, or they jump to the conclusion that these super-beings must be hostile, like that horrible Quantrell woman. I don't see that that follows. I think they'd be more inclined to be curious about us. Callous too, perhaps, as we are towards ants. But I doubt if they'd regard us as being worth interfering with.'

'If we become a nuisance . . .' Sico said in a dead voice and let the suggestion complete itself in our imaginations.

'Yes. Then the comparison might not be with ants, but with — well, woodworm, or flour weevils.' Lenister wiped his glasses absently. 'But how can we guess what might constitute nuisance value to a mind of that order?'

The more I learned of this lunatic new cosmos, the less I liked it.

'Their power terrifies me,' Graubmayer muttered. 'The idea of them looking out of their own universe into ours — if that's what they are doing — why, it's fantastic!'

'Does any of this make sense to you, Drummond?' Lenister demanded.

'Sense?' I echoed. 'No, but I can see a chain of reasoning which would explain what's happened very neatly. Perhaps our unmanned shot across the solar system was what first attracted them to our next-door universe, like seeing a mouse scuttle across the kitchen floor. So when *Starventure* intruded into their kind of space they were watching for it. They might have studied it during the journey, gathering information about the crew, so that when it re-emerged near Earth they were able to — well, borrow their bodies.'

'Yes, that's more or less the same conclusion we were coming to,' Graubmayer rumbled.

'Then obviously we've got to locate the crew's own bodies, down on Earth!' I was sweating, thinking how well it was possible to scatter sixty people across the continents in a full week.

'Of course!' Sico rapped. 'But you realize we were not immediately told of the appearance of members of the crew on Earth. We weren't even informed about your seeing your brother until — oh, three or four days afterwards!'

Defensively, I said, 'But I didn't make a secret of it, you know. In fact I was so startled I walked straight into the UN press office. And something is finally being done to check out these stories, you know.'

'Thank heaven!' Sico tensed. 'Who is responsible for it?'

'A colleague of mine, Brian Watchett. He volunteered last night to take charge of the search for the' — I hesitated, because the turn of phrase was so eerie — 'crew's bodies.'

'When we do track them down,' Graubmayer said gloomily, 'I don't like to think what we may find inside.'

There were two more confrontations, lasting longer than the first and for both of us even harder to face. Once I'd accepted that this was indeed Leon, the idea of him being trapped in an artificial inhuman form by some unimaginable super-science became intolerable. And for him, of course, it was unspeakably frustrating to realize that even though he had convinced me of his identity I couldn't in my turn convince the psychologists.

I was so exhausted after the second meeting I asked to be allowed to sleep for a while and was assigned a spare cabin aboard one of the ferries. I had slept in space previously without the recurrent falling-dreams which often wake up novices and expected to be tired enough to do so again, but in the end I was compelled to resort to forced-sleep again, because every time I shut my eyes I kept seeing visions of Leon as he used to be.

For the second and third meetings, Sico and Graubmayer briefed me beforehand with lists of questions they wanted me to slip into the conversation. As far as I could tell from the pattern they implied, they were struggling to find out whether Leon's new body had entrained changes in his personality subtler than I could detect by simply listening to him talk. That made sense, since Leon had himself referred to one such change when he cited his inability to feel different in spite of his extra limbs.

But what Graubmayer seemed to place his greatest faith

in was the question of sexuality. To reduce the risk of emotional friction between the members of the crew, the sex drive had been deliberately depressed, by tranquillizers and hormone treatments. In consequence everyone aboard *Starventure* had an extraordinarily low index of involvement with sex. But the repression was only a surface phenomenon. Underneath they must remain — if they ever had been — members of a vigorous bisexual species, and if we were dealing with aliens rather than transferred personalities, he argued, here was where their pretence was most likely to wear thin.

Null subject. I heard Leon's words in memory and shuddered.

Sico's line of attack was related to Graubmayer's, but he was primarily concerned at present with aggressive tendencies. I gathered that he was deliberately needling the crew, one by one, after analyzing their psychological records and computing approximately when they might be expected to lose their tempers. Being held effectively prisoners aboard the ship when they'd been looking forward to a hero's welcome home itself was fraying their nerves; he hoped to discover, he said, whether their breaking-point matched his predictions, whether they were possessed of inhuman — by implication, non-human — patience, or whether in fact they were likely to develop overt enmity.

I hoped not to be up here in the ship when the first of his results came in. So far, however, he admitted he'd been unable to distinguish between this non-human patience he was looking for, and apathy accountable by the aftermath of shock. Most of the crew, like Leon, were on the surface as eager to reach a definite conclusion about themselves as he was.

I was limp with relief when it came time for the ferry to depart. Lenister, by contrast, was half minded to beg permission for a longer stay. There were two reasons why he reluctantly refrained: the limited facilities up here wouldn't allow anyone to mount a third research programme as elaborate as Graubmayer's or Sico's, and both the latter had as much routine help as they needed; and someone must, after all, analyze the data being amassed up here with better computers than could be shipped up to orbit. Al ready, in a single day, he said he'd accumulated enough fresh material to keep his groundside staff busy for a week.

I'd gone to the lock as early as I reasonably could, and put on my suit. I debated with myself whether to go to Leon's cabin and say goodbye, but the third of our meetings had been harrowing for us both, and I decided against it. Hanging in air in the corridor near the lock, I waited impatiently for Lenister to arrive and accompany me aboard the ferry.

Suddenly there was a commotion. A stream of people from the after ferry hold came diving up the corridor, whitefaced. I jammed myself back against the bulkhead to get out of their way, hearing shouts from the noseward direction. Reflexive alarm started me in the wake of the others.

The slow curve of the corridor ensured that only about fifty feet of it were in clear sight at one time. I'd gone about that distance when I saw that the people who had passed me had met another group coming from the forward ferry hold and were turning along the branch passage leading to the mid-ships external vision blister. Both Sico and Graubmayer were among them. Glancing behind me, I saw there was another batch of half a dozen excited people approaching, including Rokossovsky.

I crowded along with everyone else into the vision blister. I'd had no chance to ask anyone what was going on, but the moment I entered the blister, I knew anyway.

Spanning a third of the visible sky, which in the ship's present attitude was centred on the constellation Argo, was a monster.

It was like Leon, and like the Quito monster, and like the Santadonna monster, and different from all of them. The first difference to strike me was its colour. It was much greener than the earlier ones, and there were only a few small areas which showed black and vacant because they were radiating in the invisible ultra-violet. I was immediately chilled by the horrible suspicion that the things might be getting better at peering into our space, and energies of longer wavelength were passing through whatever fantastic window they had opened on the solar system.

Before I'd had more than a quick glimpse, however, the blister became so crowded that my view was blocked. Crossing and recrossing, a tangle of arms and legs flailed in

111

the air as everyone struggled for a sight of the monster. An authoritative voice — I couldn't see whose — rang out, ordering everyone without a specific task to pull back against the in-ship bulkheads. Mechanical whirring began as automatic recorders were triggered; *Starventure's* vision blisters were all equipped for spectroanalysis in every band of radiant energy.

Silent now, we obeyed, leaving a small group of technicians floating close to the busy machines. Into this sudden hush an announcement crackled from the PA system.

'Report from Earthside! Naked-eye observation shows nothing, repeat nothing, in the indicated direction. Scans with infra-red, ultra-violet and radio frequency 'scopes are being arranged as quickly as possible.'

All around me I saw grim-set mouths, wide eyes and wondering expressions. What could it be out there, insubstantial as though painted soap-bubble thin on the fabric of space — this monster whose mouth might open to devour *Starventure* like a toad gulping a fly?

It began to fade within minutes. Just as it was vanishing the voice from the PA blared out again.

'All Earthside reports are negative, repeat negative. Nothing can be detected from down below.'

I turned away with the eel-like wriggle I was finally getting the knack of, and found myself face to face with Lenister.

'We ought to get along to the ferry,' he said. 'It's time to go.'

'Yes,' I said. 'It's time to go.'

18

Dreamlike, the return flight slipped by me. Not the scream of air on the hull as we made our braking passes; not the way the racing world vanished in a cloud of flame as the forward rockets blazed; nothing could break my mood of solitary desolation. It was only after I had mechanically climbed down from the electric trolley which this time had been on hand to fetch us back from the ferry that I snapped back to normal awareness.

What triggered the reaction was the sight of Brian Watchett standing impatiently beside the orrery in the briefing room.

'Brian!' I called, hurrying towards him. 'Have you heard anything from Carmen?'

'Who?' he countered, and my heart sank. 'Oh, – your girlfriend, you mean. No, I haven't seen her. Listen, though, David! We've found your brother!'

It was my turn to be at a loss. For long seconds the words made no sense. As far as I was concerned, Leon was up at the starship. Then I reacted.

'You mean he's been seen again? By whom? Where?'

'We have a report from Athens, Greece. He was recognized there a few hours ago. I've been half-killing myself with waiting for you to get back.'

He jabbed his finger at my spacekit. 'Lose that stuff, quickly, and meet me in Cassiano's office as fast as you can. Don't waste time asking questions now – you'll have plenty of time when we're on our way.'

It was all set up: a fast car to the hotel to collect my gear and the mail that was waiting for me, then a UN plane – a ramjet stratodiver – specially assigned to Brian for his project. Things had been happening with incredible rapidity since I left for orbit.

Correction: not incredible. With Brian's determination reinforced by the spreading mood of alarm among all Earth's top officials, it was rather to be expected.

After a period of cudgeling his brains, he had come up with a simple but ingenious means of enlisting the public's aid in his search without revealing the truth. He had had it announced that there were impostors about, claiming to be members of the starship's crew – confidence tricksters, in effect, some of whom were alleged to have been planning for this moment for years, to have undergone plastic surgery and voice alteration in the hope of deceiving even the families of the men they were imitating.

Some of them – so said the official handout which Brian showed me in the car – had already tried to trade on people's credulity. Others were lying low, awaiting a chance to emerge. Anyone who saw a man whose resem-

113

blance to one of the crew was too complete to be coincidence was therefore asked to notify the authorities straight away.

The handout included a complete set of passport-size pictures of the crew, plus fingerprints, descriptions and lists of mannerisms and distinguishing marks. It was a remarkably thorough job considering how quickly it must have been prepared.

'But that's only the half of it,' Brian said. 'Last night we put clips of those crewmen — like Leon and Hermanos — who have already been reported, on a worldwide TV linkup, and almost at once we started getting these reports from Athens.'

'Is there anything to them?' I demanded.

'We're going to have to find that out when we get there.'

Which was true enough. I turned my attention to the mail I'd collected from my hotel. There was only one item of importance: a 'faxed note from Hank Sandler. I read the opening paragraph, and that was enough.

'You are on retainer for Solar Press to cover the landing of *Starventure's* crew. The enormous public interest at present in this story led us to expect that you would honour our contract. We have heard nothing from you for more than a day, and according to our associate Manuel Segura of Prensam you have in fact left Quito on another story without informing us. We must therefore conclude that you wish to terminate our agreement. Our legal advisors are of the opinion . . .'

And so on. Sandler must have been boiling with rage; it was only when he was very angry that he used such stilted turns of phrase. I balled the letter up and stuffed it into the car's waste slot.

'Did Hank decide to fire you?' Brian asked.

I nodded and shrugged.

'I'm sorry. I talked to him last night and tried to calm him down, but he was too damned furious to listen to reason. Don't worry about him suing for breach of contract, though. I told Kaye and Don, and we agreed that if he tried to push it that far we'd resign *en bloc*.'

'Thanks,' I said, but I couldn't keep the bitterness from showing in my voice. All my working life I'd done my best to tell the truth to the world. Now for the first time ever I was engaged in promoting what I believed to be a justifiable lie, and this was the immediate result.

There was a grey silence until the car pulled in at the airport gates. Then Brian said, 'I hope to heaven it really is your brother we find in Athens.'

'That's exactly the point,' I said. 'It won't be. It'll be someone — or *something* — using his body.'

Paling, Brian stared at me. 'What did you find up there, then?'

'I'll tell you on the plane,' I said. 'And it won't make you any happier than I am.'

But on the plane I managed to catch a couple of hours' natural sleep, and when we arrived I felt a good deal better. We were, of course, expected. There were police waiting, who piled us into a car and escorted us with shrieking sirens along the coast road from the airport. That brief journey was like being in a crazy time machine. The road ran beside the sun-dappled Mediterranean, so blue and beautiful in the summer sunlight it was hard to credit that it was so polluted one dared not swim in it without an aqualung, and on the inland side children came running to the windows of handsome post-turn-of-the-century villas to wave at our noisy cavalcade. Then we made a sharp right turn towards the centre of Athens, and a broad boulevard stepped on three levels carried us a couple of miles. Ahead I saw a carefully preserved group of ruins: the Arch of Hadrian, nearly two thousand years old. A police car was parked nearby, and our driver slowed to wave at a man standing beside it. The man gave a thumbs-up sign in reply, and we accelerated again.

'He is still in view of the police,' explained the Greek who had taken us in charge at the airport.

'Where is he?' I said.

'In the Odeion Herodou Attikou. It is the classical theatre below the Acropolis.'

The time machine was still at work; now we went jolting down the narrow streets of the Plaka, which apparently hadn't changed in the past century. It was mid-afternoon, so there were few people about.

'It is the third day he has been there,' our escort went on. 'Of course, we knew what was happening, but there was no reason to be interested until we heard from Quito about these impostors who have been seen. We do not know how

115

it all began, but the first day there were nearly two hundred people who gathered to listen, and yesterday twice as many. Today the Odeion is almost full.'

'What's he doing?' I demanded.

'He talks. He answers questions from the crowd. But I'm afraid I have not listened to him myself.'

'Have you any idea who he really is?' Brian asked, in pursuance of his story that this man must be a fake.

'None. Though we know various things about him. He has not used the name of "Drummond", but when people in the crowd address him I understand that they call him "Leon". Last week he came here on a plane from the United States. He has been remembered by people who saw him in the museum on the Acropolis the day after he arrived. He has bought a great many books in several languages. He has asked several people about our famous ancient philosophers. He has visited the Stoa which is rebuilt near the Acropolis, and he has been seen sitting on a broken pillar and thinking in the sun. And now, suddenly, he has begun to act as a philosopher himself. And they listen!'

The car came to a halt just behind an identical one which was parked at the end of the winding stone-flagged path up the magnificent side of the Acropolis itself. I'd visited it before when I was covering a scientific congress here, many years ago. But I'd forgotten what a terrific impact it had, crowned with its supreme architectural masterpiece, the Parthenon.

Our driver and his companion leaped out to speak to a senior police officer sitting in the other car. On hearing that we'd arrived, he also got out and came to greet us. He spoke good English.

'The man who is posing as your brother is in the Odeion at the moment,' he said. 'It is very hot in the sun, but there are seven hundred people listening to him. It is probable that he is preparing some confidence trick, as has been suggested. Perhaps mystical knowledge from the stars, or some such rubbish.'

I licked my lips, glancing up the hill towards the entrance of the theatre. From here it was not possible to see the vast crowd which had assembled.

'Please come with us ' the policeman invited me. 'Come to a place where you can look down and recognize him. If he is indeed disguised as your brother, we shall be able to arrest him for questioning. And he will need to explain himself very cleverly!' He reached through the window of his own car to retrieve a pair of binoculars from the seat.

'This way!'

There were two shocks awaiting me at the top of the steep path leading to the Odeion. The first was the one I was prepared for. I knew, even before I was handed the binoculars for a closer look, that this was my brother's physical form. It was like a blow in the stomach to see that familiar face, hear that familiar voice ringing out over the audience.

The second was entirely different. He was speaking Russian. I'd never gained more than a halting knowledge of that language, but — as I remembered when I thought about it — Leon must of course have become reasonably fluent in it, because of the volume of scientific literature published in it.

'There are many Russian tourists here this afternoon,' the policeman whispered to me. 'A group of about a hundred came from Tashkent yesterday.'

I nodded, looking around. This was an amphitheatre of purest classical form — indeed, for the past century or so the ancient dramas had been performed here every summer. On the steep-ranked stone benches, little more than steps, were at least the seven hundred people I'd been told of — native Athenians and tourists intermingled, filling all but the topmost rows. And at the head of every aisle leading down between the seats there were uniformed police sweating in the afternoon heat.

The policeman tapped me on the shoulder. 'Mr Drummond, is he disguised as your brother?'

'Ah . . . Yes,' I said. 'He looks exactly like my brother.' And wondered how much of a truth that was.

The Leon-person, standing on the low checker-tiled stage — hardly more than a dais, in fact — paused. At once a question was shouted at him, and he began to answer at length, still in Russian.

'Then we can proceed,' the policeman said with grim satisfaction. 'Would you like to accompany me when I make the arrest Mr Drummond?'

'I'd rather not,' I said.

'As you like.' He drew a whistle from the pocket of his

uniform, and poised it to blow.

'Be careful,' I whispered, thinking of what might be hiding behind the Leon-face. 'He's —'

Brian nudged me, as though warning me to hold my tongue, and I abandoned the sentence.

'We shall be very careful,' promised the policeman. 'I have brought here my most experienced men.'

He blew the whistle. At the signal, the men standing at the top of every aisle started to march in step towards the stage. Behind the Leon-person, from the actor's entrances, half a dozen more police emerged.

The blowing of the whistle had attracted the attention of most of the audience. Now almost everyone took notice, and a babble of curious questions broke out.

Stolidly the police closed on my 'brother'. He showed no reaction, apart from breaking off his discourse and looking at the encircling men with quizzical half-smile. That smile belonged to Leon too. The recognition was heartbreaking.

From the edge of the stage, the officer who had been beside me turned and addressed the crowd, first in Greek, then English; he would presumably have gone on in any other tongue he knew, but before he had completed his second version of the announcement, I could smell the anger of the crowd beginning to rise.

He had told them that this man was using the name of one of *Starventure's* crew and had copied his appearance, but that the real Leon Drummond was still up in orbit; that he was going to take the impostor for questioning —

'*Ochi! Ochi!*' the shouting began quickly: 'No! No!' And as the sense of his words reached more people, the tumult swelled, in English, Italian, Russian: 'No, let him go on! We want to hear more!'

The moment the first policeman laid hands on 'Leon', the anger exploded, and the stage was swamped by a furious mob. It took fully ten minutes for order to be restored . . . and by then, nobody knew how, the creature in my brother's body had disappeared.

19

When tempers had cooled to the point where it was possible to think coherently again, a search was mounted, though I was already sickly certain it would fail. Some of the police fanned out around the approaches to the Acropolis, while others radioed to alert the entire local force and ordered roadblocks and street-corner checkpoints to be set up. Meantime, furious, the officer in charge questioned members of the audience whom he had managed to detain on the convenient charge of obstructing his men in the execution of their duty.

It became clear at once that it was no good asking about the disappearance of 'Leon'. For one thing, the people being interrogated seemed to be perfectly honest in denying that they'd seen where he went — the confusion had been tremendous. For another, even an ordinary criminal could fade into the mazes of the Plaka and evade anything short of a house-to-house search by a small army. And this creature we were seeking might well be able to take to escape routes where we had no hope of following . . .

Attempting to salvage something from the fiasco, Brian closely questioned as many as possible of the people who had been listening to 'Leon', hoping for clues to the nature of the body's present occupant. From the Russians who had occupied most of the front rows of the theatre, we could learn little. Sullenly they pretended to miss the point, or not to understand what was being said to them. I reflected that they were a people with long memories, inclined to distrust policemen.

From some of the Athenians, however, we got better results, and particularly from a pleasant-mannered elderly woman named Iris Argyros, a language teacher and amateur Greek classicist. She seemed dreadfully upset to find herself under arrest, but clung doggedly to the belief that it was all due to a misunderstanding, and was voluble in her attempts to persuade us that this was so.

'It was like being transported to the Golden Age!' she

declared, eyes glowing. 'I've dreamed all my life of sitting at the feet of another Socrates and hearing him expound the nature of the world with crystalline logic. And today my dream has come true!'

'But what was he talking about?' Brian pressed.

'Much of the time today he was speaking Russian, and I didn't understand everything he said. But I speak English, as you hear, and he also addressed us in that language.' She bit her lower lip and rolled her eyes upward as though seeking inspiration. 'His arguments are impossible to summarize, because they were so rigorous, one step following another like notes of music. In any case it wasn't the substance of what he was saying that impressed me so, but the beautiful logic and the vivid metaphors and analogies which he —'

'Yes, but *what was he talking about?*' Brian was running out of patience.

'Oh!' She looked vaguely surprised. 'The nature of truth, mankind's place in the universe, our habit of forming inflexible opinions and clinging to them because admitting we can ever have been wrong offends our vanity and our self-esteem. In particular, he was demonstrating how scientific orthodoxy can conflict with the concept of objective truth.'

Brian gave me a blank look. Drawing me aside, he asked in a low tone, 'David, how do you imagine he held his audience with such dry stuff as that?'

'God knows,' I muttered. 'I've spent my working life trying to pre-package ideas for the great and wonderful public, but I've never tackled philosophical concepts of that order. I wouldn't dare.'

Brian clenched his fists. 'If only those knuckle-headed police had thought of recording what he said!' he exclaimed.

But they hadn't, and apart from a handful of inferior tourist-type visual recordings which the police confiscated for us we were able to get nothing more concrete from the dozens of people we questioned. It was as though they had been spellbound, and then awakened to find the words they had heard fading like images from a dream.

Or like the — creature — which had uttered them.

As hopes of locating our quarry faded, I began to be

aware of just how much had been going on since I went up to *Starventure*. Coming on top of the shock of meeting Leon in his alien form, the news Brian had given me on the way to Athens had barely sunk in, although I'd been much impressed by his ingenious scheme to have the crew's bodies spotted. Now I found him putting in A-1 priority calls to Quito, New York and Tokyo, issuing orders to top UN officials to track down other crewmen about whom there had been rumours, while I sat exhaustedly in the background.

When he was finished with that, I asked him for more details of his project and learned that he had not only been given an emergency staff to help Chambord maintain the official lie we'd concocted, but also a temporary UN rank one step below Assistant Secretary General, at Cassiano's special request. Apart from the cover story and tracking rumoured appearances of the crewmen, he was also supposed to damp down speculation about sky-monsters, and this, he assured me wryly, was by far the toughest aspect of the job.

To my surprise, there was even yet no panic, as I'd half-expected. There was, however, a continual nervous argument in progress the world over, especially among scientists, and every paper and news bulletin was laying heavy emphasis on the fact that the experts were giving the problem their fullest attention. For years I'd done my best to discourage people from leaving it to the experts; now I was profoundly glad I hadn't succeeded.

But the present situation wouldn't last. Sooner or later our nerve was bound to snap.

Brian had told me, back in Quito, that both the Secretary General and the Chairman of the General Assembly had been to confer with the scientists at the spaceport. Knowing this, I found that certain items in the news took on interesting implications. There was a debate, for instance, about the starflight budget for the coming year; it was likely to be up, not down, ostensibly to finance research into the psychological and physiological problems I'd helped Brian to invent and to fund a second flight by *Starventure* on which possible countermeasures could be tested. In fact, of course, this must be needed to fund the colossal research programme already underway, which was being blithely disguised as 'routine debriefing and medical care.'

I felt a kind of irrational, helpless anger at the sky monsters. They had so completely upset our ideas not only of ourselves but of reality! Was it because people were already failing to be fooled by official deception that so many of them were willing to listen to 'Leon'?

Cork-fashion, I bobbed and spun on a torrent of despair.

Meantime, we probably had sixty human bodies with inhuman minds at large among Earth's five billion population. Doing what? Something as innocuous as 'Leon', philosophizing to a chance-gathered audience . . . or something sinister, incomprehensible, dangerous?

Late that night, more reports came in for Brian at the Athens police headquarters on Bouboulinas Street, 'faxed from Quito by satellite relay. In a room assigned to us on the top floor, we sorted through them. There were over two dozen altogether, of which the majority were vague and tinged with hysteria. A few, however, had a ring of accuracy, and we concentrated on these. A number of respectable witnesses had described seeing Chandra Dan at a festival in the holy city of Benares; he had spoken to a vast gathering of people — by thousands where 'Leon' had addressed hundreds — and his fame had spread like wildfire, some of the papers going so far as to call him an avatar of Krishna. Wisely, the Indian police had taken no action against him, but were keeping him under observation. And another crewman whom I hadn't met, Yussuf bin Saleem, was reported in Mecca — again, attracting crowds of people and fascinating them with his preaching. (Preaching? Well, I couldn't think of a better word.)

Unfortunately the police at Mecca had been clumsier and attempted to take him in for questioning. He had vanished as 'Leon' had, under cover of a confused melee.

'What do you make of all this?' Brian snapped at me. With difficulty I ordered my muddled brain.

'I have a wild idea,' I said after a pause. It had only this instant come to me.

'I don't care how wild it is, I want to hear it.'

I leaned forward in my chair, staring at the floor. 'It's just a guess . . . but so far we have Athens, Benares, Mecca. Doesn't that hint at a pattern? All three are centres of human religious and ethical teaching. I'd say we ought to watch for more appearances in Rome, Jerusalem, and any other city from which a great teacher or a school has influenced the world.'

Brian stared as though I were talking nonsense. Maybe I was, but his expression angered me.

'Are you serious?' he demanded.

'Why in hell shouldn't I be?' I countered and cast around for reasons to convince him. They offered themselves instantly as though the whole notion had been previously forged in my subconscious. 'Look, maybe it was Mrs Argyros with her reference to Socrates which put this into my head, but regardless of where it came from it makes a cockeyed sort of sense. We've been struggling to decide why the aliens' — the term was automatic by now — 'should be acting as they are: transferring the crew's minds into new bodies, borrowing the original bodies to visit Earth. I think there's an explanation so obvious we've overlooked it!'

'I . . .' Brian hesitated. 'Yes, finish what you were going to say. I think I'm with you, and I'd love to believe you're right!'

'Figure it this way,' I said. 'We're working on the assumption that the aliens didn't know about us until we started to fire our ships through hyperspace. Now suppose we were suddenly confronted by another species that was clearly intelligent, clearly capable of considerable technical achievements: what would be the second thing about them we'd want to investigate after satisfying ourselves that they were indeed reasoning beings?'

'Their psychology,' Brian said at once. 'Most of all, their attitude towards one another, from which we could try and extrapolate their probable attitude towards ourselves.'

'Precisely. It would make all the difference to know if they looked on their fellow beings as rivals, or as friends and equals. But it wouldn't be safe, would it, to generalize about a five-billion-strong species on the strength of a sixty-person sample?'

'Of course not. To start with, the crew of a pioneering ship like *Starventure* would be completely atypical. They'd have been hand-picked for qualities not found in every member of the race — adventurousness, self-reliance, exceptional initiative.'

'Right. But you can't choose which of this other race you're going to come into contact with; you have to contact them as a species or not at all. So you'd want to know their ideals, **the** standards they're attempting to live up to. And where those standards seemed to you to be inadequate as a basis for friendly contact, you'd try to influence people in your favour before coming out into the open.'

'Is that what you think is being done to us right now?' Brian suggested. 'A sort of — well, advance PR job?'

'I don't "really think" anything,' I sighed. For a few moments I'd thought of my idea as an inspiration. Now it seemed to rest on so few crumbs of fact that it felt like a wildly optimistic guess, not a serious working hypothesis.

Brian, however, had a thoughtful expression. 'I acted far too quickly,' he muttered. 'My only excuse is that we'd had a week of no action at all. How the devil am I going to make our story about impostors square with instructions to the police to leave them completely alone? The rope to hang themselves bit, I guess . . . Well, it's definite that we're up against creatures with powers we've never dreamed of, so the less we do to offend them, the better. But where's the borderline between proper caution and open hostility in an alien mind?'

'How should I know?' I said wearily. 'I'm not even sure whether I ought to take my own idea seriously now.'

'Well, I'm going to,' Brian said with decision. 'So seriously, in fact, I'm going to 'fax Rome and Jerusalem right away and warn them to expect crewmen to show up if they haven't already done so. There's certainly an Italian on board — what's his name . . .? Ugo Martinelli, of course: I remember. And I think there's an Israeli engineer. Where's my copy of that handout I showed you?' He turned and began rifling through a stack of papers.

Suddenly, extracting the sheet he'd been looking for, he checked and gave me a sympathetic smile.

'Sorry, David. You must have been through hell up there at the ship. I didn't have any business dragging you away from Quito without a chance to rest up after the shock.'

'I'd have been blind angry if you'd set off for Athens looking for Leon's body without telling me,' I countered.

'Yes, but it's been a wild-goose chase, hasn't it? And there certainly won't be any further developments here for a while. Look, I saw the way you flaked out on the plane. I know you didn't get any sleep the night before last, and I don't imagine you slept much when you were aboard the ship. You're living on your nerves right now. Why don't you go book a hotel room and sleep the clock around? I'll keep you in touch if there's any news.'

I got up. 'Not a bad idea,' I said. 'But I'm not going to catch up on my sleep in a hotel here. I'll book a couch on a transatlantic express and head back to Quito.'

'To keep in touch at the centre of events?' Brian said. 'Or for some — ah — more personal reason?'

'A more personal reason.'

'You're quite right,' Brian nodded. 'A man should have more than one other person in the world that he's close to, and because of what's become of your brother . . . Well, never mind my giving you advice; you know it all already, I'm sure. She's a very attractive girl, your Carmen, even if she is a trifle fey. Are you thinking of marrying her?'

'Thinking,' I said bitterly. 'Right now, I don't even know if I'll find her again, and if I do find her I'm not certain I'll recognize her as the same person.'

20

One thing to be grateful for, I reflected dully as my cab rolled from the airport towards the city centre of Quito, was that we'd grown into the habit of electing supporters of the *status quo* to govern us. It was scientists, delving deep into the nature of the world, who were suffering most from having it turned topsy-turvy. For at least a little while longer we could rely on people whose attitudes were a bit more empirical, including government administrators, pretending that everything was still perfectly normal. After all, when Galileo's news broke, most people probably waited a moment to see whether the world felt any different, found it didn't, and kept right on going.

So the big panic was in the minds of the Lenisters, the Graubmayers and the Sicos. Other folk were going about their business with only occasional pauses for anxiety. Here on the Calle Carpenter, for example, one of Quito's newest and smartest shopping streets, the crowds were as thick as they always were, and only the odd glance towards the sky or short-lived look of worry betrayed the fact that —

'Stop!' I shouted at my driver. Reflex made him slam the brakes on, nearly hurling me over his shoulder. He half-turned, framing insults. I threw some bills at him, telling him to wait for me, and leaped out of the cab. Like a madman I raced up the nearest escalator to the shopping level ten feet above the trafficway. I pushed frantically between the slow-moving shoppers, calling at the top of my voice.

'Carmen! *Carmen!*'

People I jostled swung round to complain; I was already past. I caught sight of her again, twenty paces ahead, apparently not having heard me, for she was walking steadily away. Putting on a spurt which made me nearly dizzy with lack of breath in spite of the oxygen-utilization pull I'd taken before leaving my plane, I managed to catch her up and clutch at her arm.

Startled, she spun to face me. She was wearing black — an outfit I'd seen before. What I'd never seen before was dirt on her low shoes and bare feet, black rims to her fingernails, her hair hanging in a tangle on the nape of her neck as though she lacked the patience any longer to brush it smooth. She was wearing no makeup, and her eyes were even brighter than usual.

'David!' she exclaimed, and for a moment my heart hesitated. Then she gave a pleased smile. 'Oh, I've been looking everywhere for you! I called your hotel yesterday when I found Hermanos, but they said you'd gone away to Greece.'

'You found Hermanos?' I said, my mind drained to a foolish emptiness.

'Yesterday morning! I was sure I could, if I could only learn to trust my second sight. Come with me, and I'll show him to you so you'll know everything's all right, so you'll stop worrying about Leon!'

Standing here, it was my turn to be jostled and poked by passers-by. I took her hand and drew her to the side of the walk where we would be less of an obstruction. I took a deep unrewarding breath.

'I've seen Leon's body,' I said. 'I saw it in Athens.'

'His . . . body?' Her slim hand with its un-Carmenlike dirty nails went to her mouth. 'Oh, David! You mean he is dead?'

'Worse than dead,' I told her curtly. 'The body moves and speaks, but the mind inside isn't Leon – any more than the mind in what you're talking about is Hermanos.'

Her lips a little parted, her eyes fixed on my face, she shook her head. 'David, I don't understand. Who should know Hermanos better than his family – better than I?'

'You say you've seen him. Have you talked to him?'

'Yes – yes, of course!'

'Did he recognize you at once? Did his behaviour seem normal? Did he sound like your brother when he spoke?'

'Oh, he says wonderful things! You must hear him – '

'Answer my question,' I gritted. 'Did he recognize you?'

A flicker of worry came and went behind her eyes. 'It had been two years –' she began defensively.

'I thought so. He didn't know his own sister. Because the thing that moves him like a puppet on strings is *not Hermanos*, do you hear me?' I was suddenly terrified at my inability to convince her; I was suddenly afraid to trust my own memory of what had happened up at *Starventure*. 'Your brother is aboard the starship, trapped like mine in an alien body. Didn't you believe what Suvorov told us? Didn't you read in the papers or see on TV that there are impostors pretending to be – '

Like the shutter of a camera the end of a time exposure, black disbelief closed over her mind. I broke off. Nothing I could say would reach her. This was as much a stranger in a familiar body as 'Hermanos' or 'Leon'.

'Come with me, David,' she said. 'I will show you the truth.'

'Where?' I snapped. 'Where is he?'

'Come with me,' she repeated. 'If you don't see with your own eyes, you will never believe me. I don't want to say where I shall take you. I don't want strangers to come, police, people who might interfere.'

'Then . . .' My mind raced. 'Look, I have a cab waiting on the trafficway below. We can –'

'There are radios in cabs,' she cut in. 'The driver would have to say where he was going. No, David. We will walk to the place. I came to the city on foot this morning, and I shall go back the same way. It is up to you whether you come or not.'

She intended to turn away with finality: take it or leave it. But at the last moment she couldn't; she checked and glanced back with a trace of hope. The appealing light in her eyes broke through my despair.

I'd been wrong. She wasn't a stranger. She was the same Carmen. My mistake had been to imagine that I knew her well, when in fact I was perfectly aware she was the only woman I'd ever met who would go on surprising me for a lifetime, not because she would change, but because she was such a complex person. Determined, but not obstinate; fey, but not supersititous . . .*right*, in uncountably many ways.

How could I even blame her for insisting that what she had seen was her brother? Was it not more reasonable to assume that a mind could be altered by a unique experience than to think it had been displaced from its body altogether? She hadn't had the chance I'd had, to compare a personality to its mere physical envelope. In the same situation, I'd probably have clung myself to the 'common sense' explanation.

'All right,' I said. 'I'm coming with you.'

Delighted, she seized my hand in both of hers, and for a moment I almost stopped thinking I was a damned fool.

I walked beside her as obediently as a well-trained dog. She led me from the Calle Carpenter along the Calle Titov, from the glittering storefronts to the plain, rather makeshift apartment blocks of an artisan quarter which had been thrown up at the time when the spaceport began to bring fame and prosperity to this highland capital city. There were still peasant markets here; on stalls each of which prominently displayed a municipal trading licence men and women with markedly Indian features offered traditional handicrafts and foodstuffs. The crowds were as dense as those in the Calle Carpenter, but more purposeful. I sensed an air of haste.

'People seem to be going our way,' I murmured when I finally read a pattern into the flow of the throng.

'Yes. There was another angel in the sky last night.' She answered absently, as though her mind was on another subject.

'Angel?' I echoed.

She caught herself and turned a laughing face to me. 'Well, one has to give them some name, I guess!'

'Do you mean a monster, like the one we saw together

from your apartment?'

'Ah . . .' She hesitated. 'It doesn't seem — I mean it doesn't *feel* right to call them monsters. Huge shining creatures that move in the heavens — they might as well be nicknamed angels as anything else, mightn't they?'

There didn't seem to be any future in arguing that point. I tried another approach. 'Are all these people heading the way we are *because* something showed up in the sky last night?'

'Yes, of course. They are afraid. So they are going to hear Hermanos, and he will give them courage.'

'What on earth does he do for them?'

'He — talks to people. David, why ask me to describe it? In a little while you can hear for yourself!'

It was a sort of pilgrimage. The crazy time machine I'd imagined in Athens was still affecting me. We walked among stone-faced people like Aztec idols, some in modern clothing, some with a *serape* or *rebozo* tossed about them as a conscious gesture to the past. There was no definite beginning to their irregular procession; simply, when we left the city we saw many people on the road ahead, in small groups or by themselves, and others later came and followed us. I felt as conspicuous as a leper because I was so pale. Carmen's face, bearing and complexion blended in with the straggling crowd, but I was a white North American and the only Caucasian present as far as I could tell. I had a sense of isolation, of being cut off from some fundamental well of knowledge which these people accepted and would never dream of questioning.

The road deteriorated when it passed the outlying private homes and became a gravelled track winding round the shoulder of a hill. We came on people who had set out earlier and exhausted themselves, sitting by the road gathering the energy to continue. My own feet, unused to walking, began to ache, and I suspected a blister on my right heel.

'Where are we making for?' I demanded. 'A village?'

'Yes, a village. It's not far — only eight kilometers from Quito.'

Five miles. I guessed we'd covered a mile and a half since leaving the city limits. I looked around at the inhospitable landscape — to my eyes, at any rate. That time machine was

129

very efficient. The countryside seemed raw from Nature's hand; the towers of Quito, visible on glancing back, were as insubstantial as a mirage, and one could believe the wind might blow them away.

But it was the background that these people had known since childhood. Their ancestors' bones were part of this soil. Their beliefs were founded on these rocks and that oppressive sky.

Carmen's, too.

And this also was humanity's heritage. The dirt and disorder of the world were closer to us than our new, clean, sterile machines. The confusion of mountains, the tangle of forests, were more familiar than the stark blackness beyond the air, where *Starventure* had roamed.

We had deluded ourselves that we could cope up there. We had imagined we could reduce the cosmos to simple, predictable rules. I thought of the race's finest minds battling with an insoluble enigma; I thought of Leon, puzzled but tolerant, in a body wished on him by . . . all right, a miracle. A miracle is a happening contrary to natural laws, and all our law forbade this event.

Call them angels, then — why not?

The road wound, steep and stony and narrow, and the mass of people passing along it thickened as those ahead wearied and those behind grew more eager. We were almost shoulder to shoulder as we completed the journey and came in sight of the village which was our goal.

It was nothing special: a square into which the road rebouched, with an old church on one side, a blatantly new concrete building opposite which a sign identified as a library, a school also of concrete but considerably older, its walls cracking, and some sort of local government office. Behind these, houses, many thatched with reed or cane but with modern metal-framed windows set in their pale brown walls. And beyond, the fields of corn and imported grass for a few cattle to graze, and root crops which I didn't recognize. Clearly this was one of the lucky villages, touched by progress — the grass in particular was eloquent of UN aid — but it seemed to have made no difference to the people.

Most of the newcomers, moving as though completing some traditional ritual, settled down in the dusty square, taking advantage of patches of shade or spreading their *serapes* like awnings. Early arrivals had found places on the two cars parked in the square and the one and only old dirty truck; the rest had to be content with the ground.

But Carmen, catching my hand again, led me through the crowd and across the square, past the dazzling walls of the new library whose bulk dipped briefly into shadow, towards a house larger than the majority, just behind the church. On its verandah a portly priest sat in an old rocking chair talking with a slender man whose complexion exactly matched Carmen's, who wore a white shirt and loose white peasant-style trousers belted with a bright red sash.

He looked towards us and gave us a nod, his face calm and friendly. I recognized that face. It belonged to Hermanos Iglesias. After waiting which had given me a foretaste of eternity, I was going to find out what alien mind was screened behind it.

21

The appalling thing was that he also recognized me.

I had no doubt of it, the moment he glanced up from his conversation with the stout priest. The dark eyes — so like Carmen's — in his sallow face met mine, and it was as though a current flowed. I felt a sudden sense of dislocation. I was afraid I might lose my willpower and become no better than a credulous peasant.

He didn't recognize me: *David Drummond, Leon's brother*. He recognized me: *a person who knows what I am*.

My frantic struggle for self-possession climaxed in a need for speech. I said in a voice so harsh I barely knew it for my own, 'Well, *monster*, what is it you want?' I spoke in English simply because it was my mother tongue, having no idea whether this or the real Hermanos would understand me. Carmen gave a little horrified gasp and took a half-pace away from me, her eyes rounding. The priest, not catching the sense of my words but comprehending the tone of my voice, looked startled.

'Wrong question,' the alien said, with an absolutely human intonation and a human quirk of his borrowed mouth. 'The problem is: what do you want, the people of Earth? I'm having the devil's job trying to find out.'

I had expected bluster, evasion, anything but this bland acceptance of my charge. I was completely taken aback, and while I was still at a loss Hermanos had excused himself to the priest — who half-raised his right hand as though minded to pronounce a blessing but let it fall back to his lap — and stepped down from the verandah to confront me.

With an expression of intense curiosity he looked me over. 'You sound personally offended,' he said. 'Are you David Drummond, by any chance?'

I licked my lips and glanced at Carmen. She was standing apart from us, her gaze riveted on her brother's face. At last I nodded.

'Good,' the Hermanos-person said. 'We learned about you from your brother Leon, of course. Have you seen him since his return?'

I almost choked with fury, and he laid his hand on my arm, apparently much concerned. 'Is he not well? He should not be suffering in spite of what we did to him — we took great care!'

Shaking his hand off me, I forced my anger down to a level at which I could talk. 'Yes, I've seen him! I've seen both him and his stolen body!'

'And because you don't understand you are afraid, and because you're ashamed to show fear you are angry. I see.' Hermanos sounded as analytical as a psychiatrist reviewing an unusual complex of symptoms. 'Yet you're a science writer, having at least a nodding acquaintance with the whole of modern human knowledge. What a lot you've forgotten — what an *incredible* amount!'

I couldn't make sense of that, and right now I wasn't in a mood to try. I rounded on the priest, calling up all the limited Spanish I could command.

'You there!' I bawled at him. 'What do you make of this — this creature that talks like a man? He's not a man! He's a creature possessed of a devil! Why are you sitting on that verandah when out there in the plaza your flock are blaspheming against the holy angels, using their name for the monsters that appear in the sky?'

The priest, startled, looked at Hermanos and back at me.

He said, 'Sir, is the Sun affecting you? This is a good man of great wisdom. He is not possessed of any devil! And why should I stop my people talking of angels? The things in the sky are God's creatures one way or another!'

He gave a fat, toothy smile and went back to rocking his chair as though that settled the matter beyond argument.

'Hermanos,' Carmen ventured nervously, 'please forgive David. He isn't himself — he's upset, he's had a shock of some kind . . .' Her voice trailed away.

'Oh, to hell with it,' I said in English. 'The world's gone crazy and I'm sick of it. Monsters talk through the mouths of men, men turn out to be disguised as monsters, the skies are full of angels, and the hell with it *all*!'

I spun on my heel, my eyes stinging and my mind reeling.

'That's more like it,' Hermanos said behind me, his voice level. 'I'm glad you used the word "angels". Because that's exactly what they are.'

I checked and put my clenched fists to my head. My brain felt as though it might burst my skull.

'Mr Drummond, come back here,' said Hermanos. 'I want to talk to you. I want to put a hypothesis to you. In fact, I may very well want your help.'

'Help!' I repeated, and tried to laugh; the sound emerged as a manic cackle.

'That's what I said.' His voice was still calm. 'Since you've come here, you might as well benefit from the visit. What was in your mind — forcing a confession of my identity, perhaps?'

'No — what would be the use of trying to force you to do anything? You can escape by ways where we can't follow. I learned that much from the man who's pretending to be my brother.'

'Now you're rationalizing. I think the intention was at the back of your mind. Still, that's irrelevant. As you can see, I'm not keeping up any pretence. Why should I? Is there any lie I could tell which you would swallow? So further, what's the point of striding off in a bad temper?'

'Should I stay and listen to lies that you hope I *will* fall for?' I countered.

' "What is truth?" said jesting Pilate, and would not stay for an answer!' Hermanos flung up his hands. 'Are you become a race of Pilates, you human beings? Are you so obsessed with your little local treasury of empirical facts that you don't care any more about greater truths? Is the pinnacle of your ambition to grub in a yard of dirt and never turn your face to the Sun?'

He had paled with the intensity of his emotion. On the last word the muscles of his cheeks knotted and his jaw snapped shut like a bear trap.

'David!' Carmen said. 'Why won't you listen to him? Are you afraid he may make you believe what he says?' There was a hint of scorn in her voice, as though she had hoped better of the David Drummond she knew.

I yielded and moved towards the verandah. The priest, who had watched our heated exchange anxiously, gave a sigh of relief and waved me courteously to a vacant chair propped against the wall.

'Thank you,' Hermanos said. He jumped up and balanced on the waist-high wooden rail along the front of the verandah, finding a purchase for his heels so that he could lean his elbows on his knees. 'I'm a little surprised that you haven't already learned most of what I'm going to tell you from your brother. Didn't he talk to you about his experiences in hyperspace — as you call it?'

I bit my lip and glanced at Carmen, who was leaning now against one of the verandah's pillars. Feeling quite ridiculous to be discussing such a subject with someone who had admitted not being human I said, 'He told me only a little. He did say it was like ordinary space only more so. And he said we might have to treat our Einsteinian universe as a special case of the Euclidean one. But I didn't entirely follow him.'

Hermanos nodded judiciously. 'It was to be expected that mathematicians like your brother would glimpse the truth ahead of other people. But apparently it's going to take a while to digest. Well! Now I have your attention, Mr Drummond, I'd like to ask whether you're familiar with a few notions that underpin my later argument. You're an educated man, so I think you'll recognize them all. The Platonic theory of the ideal?'

I nodded warily.

'The Jungian theory of archetypes? The legends of the Golden Age, the Isles of the Blessed, the Garden of Eden?'

'Of course! But I don't see —'

'Patience, please.' He held up his hand with an alto-gether disarming grin on his face. His *borrowed* face. I had to keep reminding myself of that. 'In the course of everyday life — particularly primitive life — does a man run across such things as a perfectly straight line, a perfect right angle, a perfect half of anything?'

'Uh — no.' I shifted on my chair. I was sweating unpleasantly, as though my life depended on answering his questions. 'But surely that was one of the reasons which influenced the formulation of the theory of ideals, and it seems like a hell of a long way from angels!'

'Not so far as you might imagine. What was bothering old Plato, so I gather from what I've recently learned, was something that nowadays you appear to have given up as a bad job — to wit, why people who have never seen a truly straight line or a perfect half should be capable of formulating the concepts so clearly. Over the past century or two you seem to have become so preoccupied with your mechanical ingenuity you've given up inquiring into that.'

I was on the point of objecting, but I changed my mind. Indeed, I couldn't think of a single twenty-first-century philosopher who had seriously attacked the problem of ideals. It was thoroughly out of fashion, and I admitted as much.

'Yes, it is, and that's a shame. Because if it weren't, I've no doubt someone would have stumbled on the implications of the existence of hyperspace long before even your unmanned experimental ship flew through it. Now bear in mind what I said about legends of Golden Ages and Gardens of Eden and so on, and consider the following proposition.'

He leaned forward very earnestly.

'What you refer to as "normal space" is a very special case indeed of "hyperspace" — indeed, an *artificial distortion* of it. Human awareness isn't native to such a continuum and includes concepts which here can find no real referents. In consequence you see "through a glass darkly", and in days when the shock was fresher, attempts were made to convey a vague memory of your original reality by means of myths and legends.'

I couldn't decide whether to be more surprised by the suggestion itself, or the erudite fluency with which a self-confessed alien was presenting it. I settled for the former.

'Not native to such a continuum?' I echoed. 'What's that supposed to mean? To me it's simply noises!'

He sighed. 'Yes, that's inevitable. I've been trying to

think of some illustrations that might make it clearer. You took a terribly roundabout route back to the simplicity of hyperspace — through all kinds of mathematical detours — precisely because your awareness has been deformed along with your present environment. But imagine, though! imagine a railway train running on ideally parallel tracks. It'll run smoothly and evenly without wasting power — yes? But now imagine one of the rails a fraction out of true, so that it rubs against the wheels like a brake. The train will run slower and energy will go to waste. Transfer that to a four-dimensional space-time continuum, and picture one of the dimensions as being likewise out of true. Envisage some of the effects.'

I tried to concentrate. 'Red shift?' I said finally.

'Yes, an excellent example. But it doesn't only manifest itself over interstellar distances, this distortion. The speed of light becomes lower; the chronon — the time-quantum — is unnecessarily large; mental processes, and indeed all energy transfers, are as it were thickened and made coarse.'

In spite of my reluctance, I was beginning to call to mind arguments in support of Hermanos' fantastic proposition. I remembered what I'd been told about Chandra Dan in his new body; he'd been reacting so fast at first that they needed to process his statements through a computer because no human being could keep up with his reaction times.

Hermanos gave me a quizzical smile. 'I think my barbs are starting to fester,' he murmured. 'So your hide isn't as armour-plated as you imagined, is it? You're lucky to have such a wide range of information to draw on, though. A lot of people who don't enjoy your advantages are waiting for me out there in the plaza. Excuse me; they want me to go and talk to them.'

'What for?' I said.

'Oh . . . reassurance, I guess. They're frightened. They aren't used to the sky being full of angels. Because I don't seem to be perturbed by it, they — they look to me. Or to *us*, I should say. You said you'd seen "Leon's body" in Athens. What else was my colleague doing but talking to people and reassuring them?'

I licked my lips. 'Tell me one thing before you go,' I said. 'You keep talking about us being stuck away in a corner of

136

space-time which has been artificially deformed. You've been implying that we somehow came "from" your universe "to" ours. But what's supposed to have brought this about?'

'I can't tell you,' Hermanos said flatly. 'The referents are *so* different — even simple concepts like "to" and "from" aren't really accurate. I can only draw your attention to a very well-known myth that concerns the fall of a group of arrogant angels. There are many races in the higher continuum I'm talking about. Yours used to be one of them.'

He gave a fleeting smile and swung his legs over the rail of the verandah. 'Stay here and think it over,' he invited. 'I'll be back in a couple of hours.'

22

Carmen went after him; so did the priest, levering himself out of his chair and waddling away. I was left by myself with a myriad unanswered questions thundering around my skull.

My first impulse was to reject everything that I'd been told. But this was stupid. Faced with inexplicable events, it was more rational to accept a working hypothesis to explain them, even if one had to modify it, than to dismiss it out of hand.

I tried to calm my tumultuous mind and work out the consequences of Hermanos' idea.

First of all, then: the higher continuum which we called hyperspace was supposed to be similar to our own, only — to use Leon's phrase — 'more so.' Did this imply it would be infinite? I thought not. Rather, concepts such as distance would be of a different order. Concepts like a perfect half and a perfect straight line, which to us were mere mathematical fictions, would become not merely intuitive but literal truths.

But wait a moment. I creased my forehead achingly as I struggled through the welter of confusion besetting me. To achieve that sort of perfection, did one not need to invoke actual infinity, upward and downward from the human scale?

No, of course not! I snapped my fingers in excitement. Why hadn't Hermanos instanced Cantorian transfinite maths in his list of examples — that series of rigorously logical arguments which long ago had demonstrated that some kinds of infinity could be 'more infinite' than others?

Maybe he'd wanted to leave me something to figure out for myself.

I knew from Leon that Cantor's concepts had provided some of the basic tools for the design of *Starventure*. Einsteinian mathematics ran into a dead end at the speed of light. That fitted with the idea of a continuum where our concepts were, so to speak, magnified without being fundamentally altered. Speed, distance, anything where a time factor was involved, must take on a new meaning, though, and to guess at such new meanings was beyond me. Perhaps, once your mind had been preconditioned, you had to experience that type of reality before you could apprehend it. Leon had done his best to describe his experiences, but very little had been clear to me.

Location, separation . . . there was no end to the list of commonplace ideas which would be upset by transference into higher-order space! I wrenched my mind away from a path which led spiralling dizzily towards chaos, and tried to find an alternative approach.

Clearly it was no use trying to picture the aliens' view of their own universe, but at least it might make sense to speculate about their impression of ours. Now we'd been assuming our continuum to be finite but boundless, like the surface of a globe translated to four dimensions. If that held good, it would be possible for our entire plenum to be contained in theirs, incapable of interacting with it, so totally self-enclosed that it could be overlooked until an object — *Starventure* — burst out through its surface.

But in that case the real extent of the cosmos must be uncountable centillions of times larger than we'd ever envisaged!

My mind refused to make even an attempt to grapple with concepts on such a scale. Gratefully, I took refuge in thinking about matters that centred more directly on humanity.

After whatever inconceivable catastrophe had led to the

event which Hermanos had compared to a fall of angels, we would have been lost to the creatures of the super-universe: shut off, isolated, ignored . . . What was the word I was looking for? Of course. *Incommunicado*.

And perhaps they were happy to see us go. Whatever we had done, it could not have been a deed to be soon forgotten.

Now, though, after the passage of millennia we had struggled back from our isolation (imprisonment? self-imposed or decreed as punishment?), and reminded them of our existence. Logically, they would want to look into our cosmos and examine our solar system . . .

Now *that* was right! I remembered the worried voice I'd heard over the PA system in *Starventure's* vision blister when we had crowded to look at the latest of the monsters in the sky. I'd been struck then by the increased greenness of its appearance, as though radiation of longer wavelength was entering our kind of space. But this radiation must have been emitted from a tangential point between our distorted universe and theirs. No wonder that monster wasn't visible from Earth; no wonder the Santadonna monster, studied with such care, had no effective mass! The image we were seeing must be a less-than-paper-thin projection.

Abbott: *Flatland*. A finger through a plane surface would appear to the inhabitants of a two-dimensional universe as a rounded obstacle of insanely variable diameter.

Little by little my ability to marshal facts and analogies was drawing me back from my depression. I sat more upright in my chair, halfway to being cheerful for the first time in days. Surely it followed that if Hermanos and his 'colleagues' were prepared to talk to us, to admit their identity openly, they must have some degree of respect for us? And their fluency in the use of our languages suggested that their experience and ours could not be totally foreign to one another. Granted, they might be hiding intolerable frustration at having to employ such a clumsy mode of communication as speech — but they were taking the trouble to hide it, if so. Perhaps they perceived their universe with a fuller awareness, but it nonetheless might contain familiar objects: matter, energy, stars, planets and moons . . .

Once, much more than a century ago, Haldane had

speculated about the subjective realities experienced by other species: not only those close to us, such as dogs whose world is dominated by scent, but those with which we have little more in common than the planet we both live on — barnacles, for example, and bees. To a bee, he argued, a concept of 'duty' might be as concrete as our notion of, say, solidity.

Somewhere along those lines one might make a stumbling approach towards truth.

And, granting all this, one could see why Hermanos did not prevaricate when I challenged him. What could *they* have to fear from us, trapped in an inferior universe and constrained to follow twisted lines in the mistaken belief that they were straight? They could do anything to us without our preventing them, down to and including lifting the fragile web of personality out of one body and into another, as neatly as mechanical components, simply so that they could study us at first hand.

Yes, but . . . Having studied us, what did they intend to do?

It was approaching sunset when I grew tired of waiting by myself and walked round the side of the church back to the plaza. People were preparing to leave. Some farsighted peddlers had obtained a supply of wax torches for the return trip — of course, here on the equator darkness would come like a curtain falling — and there was a brisk trade in them at the far side of the square. Another enterprising young man was selling tortillas and a kind of enchilada to those who had forgotten to bring any food.

Hermanos was standing by the latter's stall, eating and talking to a succession of inquirers. Carmen and the priest were listening intently. I stood a few paces away until there was a break in the conversation; then Hermanos excused himself and turned to me with a twinkle in his eye.

'Well?' he said. 'Have you come to any conclusions this afternoon?'

I told him about them as baldly as I could.

'Very good,' he approved. 'If you'll allow me to make a suggestion . . .? Make this the subject of your next book. You'll be famous because of it, but that's incidental. The truth itself is what's important.'

'Yes, of course, but . . .'

'But what?' Hermanos cocked his head.

'But I still don't know what you're going to do!'

He looked surprised. 'What would you expect us to do? Leave, of course. Return these borrowed bodies to their original owners —'

Carmen gave a stifled exclamation, and he turned to her. 'Yes, I'm afraid what David told you is true,' he said kindly. 'I'm not in fact your brother — but don't worry! The next time you see this face Hermanos Iglesias will be back in charge of it.' He gave a pleasant chuckle which took all the eldritch implications out of his words.

'But do you mean you're *just* going to leave?' I insisted. 'You're not going to — well, keep in touch with us?'

'What happens from now on isn't up to us,' he said. Suddenly he was as stern as a judge, and no longer seemed to be a mere young man, slim, lightly built, quiet-voiced. 'The rest, I'm afraid, is your affair. There will be no more monsters in the sky after tonight. There will be no more people who look like people and are not. We shall wait. You must act. If you want to. You may not want to. You may be content in your little puddle, in which case there will be no more visits to the stars. You will be too afraid.'

'Act!' I cried. 'How? Tell us how!'

'Why should I? Work it out! After all, we didn't wish this fate on you. You brought it on yourselves.'

'What did we do?'

'That we will never tell you — *human*. Fortunately you seem to have forgotten; if you hadn't, we would prevent you from returning to us by closing the only possible path. You realize I or any of my kind could smash one of your puny starships more easily than you can swat a fly? But let that be. It's not important. We who remember what you did will keep the memory to ourselves, so that you may with luck escape the temptation to try it again.'

There was a silence that embraced only him, me, Carmen; the priest had gone bustling to talk with believers in the departing crowd. Yet it seemed to smother the world.

Hermanos broke it. He clapped me on the arm and gave a broad grin. 'Even if we won't help, you can be certain we won't hinder you. You've improved since we last saw you, you know. I hope very much to welcome you back with us one day.'

'You don't mean *me*,' I said.

'No, I don't mean you.' He hesitated. 'It will probably take twenty thousand years.'

While I was still lost in the contemplation of two hundred centuries, he was gone.

Rousing, I looked around in amazement. Darkness had fallen, and the four pole-mounted lights at the corners of the square showed only Carmen and the last few stragglers on their way towards Quito.

'Where did he go?' I snapped at her.

'I don't know!' she whispered. 'David, I'm afraid! He wasn't my brother — you were right after all. But I don't see how, I don't understand!'

Beseechingly, she caught at my hand and stared up at my face as though to read an answer there.

I had nothing to say. I put my arm round her shoulders; feeling her tremble, I began automatically to urge her after the others taking the Quito road, and she followed docilely. As soon as we had left the glare of the village's lights, we could see the stars and — like stars on Earth — the dozens of wavering torches that traced the curves of the road.

At intervals, people raised their heads to scan the sky. But there were no angels tonight, or any other night. There was only the glinting diamond of *Starventure*, orbiting between horizon and eclipse.

A symbol of the future. A symbol of the wrong future.

I grew aware that Carmen was weeping soundlessly, like a frightened child alone in the dark. I drew her closer, wishing that I could weep too — for our lost glory and our lost conceit. We had opened Pandora's box, and all the evils had gone out into the world, and nothing was left to us but hope.

Gradually, though, as the irregular procession wound through the chilly evening, I began to think of talking to Leon in his right shape, and arguing with him, and explaining that there was work to be done, and that spark of hope flared up like one of the torches ahead, not driving back the gloom but showing at least that there was a way forward.

FICTION

GENERAL

☐ Chains	Justin Adams	£1.25
☐ Secrets	F. Lee Bailey	£1.25
☐ Skyship	John Brosnan	£1.65
☐ The Free Fishers	John Buchan	£1.50
☐ Huntingtower	John Buchan	£1.50
☐ Midwinter	John Buchan	£1.25
☐ A Prince of the Captivity	John Buchan	£1.25
☐ The Eve of St Venus	Anthony Burgess	£1.10
☐ Nothing Like the Sun	Anthony Burgess	£1.50
☐ The Memoirs of Maria Brown	John Cleland	£1.25
☐ The Last Liberator	John Clive	£1.25
☐ Wyndward Fury	Norman Daniels	£1.50
☐ Ladies in Waiting	Gwen Davis	£1.50
☐ The Money Wolves	Paul Erikson	£1.50
☐ Rich Little Poor Girl	Terence Feely	£1.50
☐ Fever Pitch	Betty Ferm	£1.50
☐ The Bride of Lowther Fell	Margaret Forster	£1.75
☐ Forced Feedings	Maxine Herman	£1.50
☐ Savannah Blue	William Harrison	£1.50
☐ Duncton Wood	William Horwood	£1.95
☐ Dingley Falls	Michael Malone	£1.95
☐ Gossip	Marc Olden	£1.25
☐ Buccaneer	Dudley Pope	£1.50
☐ An Inch of Fortune	Simon Raven	£1.25
☐ The Dream Makers	John Sherlock	£1.50
☐ The Reichling Affair	Jack Stoneley	£1.75
☐ Eclipse	Margaret Tabor	£1.35
☐ Pillars of the Establishment	Alexander Thynn	£1.50
☐ Cat Stories	Stella Whitelaw	£1.10

WESTERN — BLADE SERIES by Matt Chisholm

☐ No. 5 The Colorado Virgins	85p
☐ No. 6 The Mexican Proposition	85p
☐ No. 7 The Arizona Climax	85p
☐ No. 8 The Nevada Mustang	85p
☐ No. 9 The Montana Deadlock	95p
☐ No. 10 The Cheyenne Trap	95p
☐ No. 11 The Navaho Trail	95p
☐ No. 12 The Last Act	95p

WESTERN — McALLISTER SERIES by Matt Chisholm

☐ McAllister and the Spanish Gold	95p
☐ McAllister on the Commanche Crossing	95p
☐ McAllister Never Surrenders	95p
☐ McAllister and the Cheyenne Trap	95p

SCIENCE FICTION

☐ Times Without Number	John Brunner	£1.10
☐ The Dancers of Arun	Elizabeth A. Lynn	£1.50
☐ Watchtower	Elizabeth A. Lynn	£1.10

WAR

☐ The Andersen Assault	Peter Leslie	£1.25
☐ Killers under a Cruel Sky	Peter Leslie	£1.25
☐ The Serbian Triangle	Peter Saunders	£1.10
☐ Jenny's War	Jack Stoneley	£1.25

FICTION

HORROR/OCCULT/NASTY

☐ Death Walkers	Gary Brandner	£1.00
☐ Hellborn	Gary Brandner	£1.25
☐ The Howling	Gary Brandner	£1.00
☐ Return of the Howling	Gary Brandner	£1.25
☐ The Sanctuary	Glenn Chandler	£1.00
☐ The Tribe	Glenn Chandler	£1.10
☐ Croak	Robin Evans	£1.10
☐ Blood Island	James Farber	£1.35
☐ Curse	Daniel Farson	95p
☐ Transplant	Daniel Farson	£1.00
☐ Rattlers	Joseph L. Gilmore	£1.00
☐ Slither	John Halkin	£1.00
☐ The Wicker Man	Hardy & Shaffer	£1.25
☐ The Skull	Shaun Hutson	£1.25
☐ The Beast Within	Edward Levy	£1.25
☐ Parasite	Richard Lewis	£1.00
☐ Spiders	Richard Lewis	£1.00
☐ The Web	Richard Lewis	£1.10
☐ Gate of Fear	Lewis Mallory	£1.00
☐ The Nursery	Lewis Mallory	£1.10
☐ The Summoning	John Pintoro	95p
☐ Bloodthirst	Mark Ronson	£1.00
☐ Ghoul	Mark Ronson	95p
☐ Ogre	Mark Ronson	95p
☐ The Scourge	Nick Sharman	£1.00
☐ Deathbell	Guy N. Smith	£1.00
☐ Doomflight	Guy N. Smith	£1.10
☐ Entombed	Guy N. Smith	£1.25
☐ Locusts	Guy N. Smith	95p
☐ Manitou Doll	Guy N. Smith	£1.10
☐ Satan's Snowdrop	Guy N. Smith	£1.00
☐ The Specialist	Jasper Smith	£1.00
☐ The Offering	Gerald Suster	£1.25
☐ The Scar	Gerald Suster	£1.25

HAMLYN WHODUNNITS

☐ Some Die Eloquent	Catherine Aird	£1.25
☐ The Case of the Abominable Snowman	Nicholas Blake	£1.10
☐ The Widow's Cruise	Nicholas Blake	£1.25
☐ The Worm of Death	Nicholas Blake	95p
☐ Tour de Force	Christianna Brand	£1.10
☐ King and Joker	Peter Dickinson	£1.25
☐ A Lonely Place to Die	Wessle Ebersohn	£1.10
☐ Gold from Gemini	Jonathan Gash	£1.10

NAME ....

ADDRESS ....

....

Write to Hamlyn Paperbacks Cash Sales, PO Box 11, Falmouth, Cornwall TR10 9EN.

Please indicate order and enclose remittance to the value of the cover price plus:

U.K.: Please allow 45p for the first book plus 20p for the second book and 14p for each additional book ordered, to a maximum charge of £1.63.

B.F.P.O. & EIRE: Please allow 45p for the first book plus 20p for the second book and 14p per copy for the next 7 books, thereafter 8p per book.

OVERSEAS: Please allow 75p for the first book and 21p per copy for each additional book.

Whilst every effort is made to keep prices low it is sometimes necessary to increase cover prices and also postage and packing rates at short notice. Hamlyn Paperbacks reserve the right to show new retail prices on covers which may differ from those previously advertised in the text or elsewhere.